ONE AFTERNOON, Rebecca and Eric Walker watch as their father is calmly driven away by three dark-suited men. "Who are they?" Rebecca asks. "Police," Eric says. "What did he do?" "Embezzled."

Their father chooses to await his trial in prison, leaving the family to auction off their grand mansion on Long Island Sound without him to repay the millions of dollars owed the clients of Walker & Lutrec. Then, just days before the trial, Mrs. Walker, frail and aristocratic, is found wandering the streets of Old Greenwich in the middle of the night wearing a taffeta formal from her high school days.

In a small apartment above Aikens' Drugstore, the Walker children band together. They masquerade unity and well-being; to fight off their "sympathetic" neighbors who now see them as charity cases; and to resist their own odd impulses.

Eric, a medical student, succumbs to his many imagined illnesses. Sarah, still in high school, runs away to New York and a career, she thinks, with a famous ballet company. Eliza, the youngest, follows close on Rebecca's heels every minute. Rebecca is the "good girl," Yale-bound in the fall but, for now, running the house, paying the bills, vehemently defending her father long after the other Walker children have stopped doing so. Then suddenly, Rebecca, the dependable one, loses control on the day of her father's trial.

The Masquerade, Susan Shreve's finest young adult novel, is really the story of Rebecca, the "best-all-around," who abandons the careful mask of respectability in a critical town. But she discovers that her wild jaunts until sunrise with a tough and dangerous young crowd *do* have a purpose. Only when she is able to look beyond their masquerade does she begin to sort out her life.

By Susan Shreve

ADULT
A Fortunate Madness
A Woman Like That
Children of Power

BOOKS FOR YOUNG READERS
The Nightmares of Geranium Street
Loveletters
Family Secrets
The Masquerade

THE
MASQUERADE

a novel / Susan Shreve

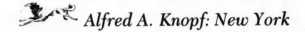 *Alfred A. Knopf: New York*

THIS IS A BORZOI BOOK
PUBLISHED BY ALFRED A. KNOPF, INC.

10 9 8 7 6 5 4 3 2 1

Library of Congress Cataloging
in Publication Data

Shreve, Susan Richards.
The masquerade.
Summary: When their father is jailed for
embezzlement and their mother suffers a
nervous breakdown, four young people try
to cope with the many changes in their
lives and the new responsibilities
thrust upon them.
[1. Family problems—Fiction.
2. Self-reliance—Fiction]
I. Title PZ7.S55915Ch 1980 [Fic] 79–20073
ISBN 0–394–84142–5
ISBN 0–394–94142–X lib. bdg.

Jacket illustration by Ben Stahl

for
Elizabeth and Jane,
good girls

ONE AFTERNOON, Rebecca and Eric Walker watch as their father is calmly driven away by three dark-suited men. "Who are they?" Rebecca asks. "Police," Eric says. "What did he do?" "Embezzled."

Their father chooses to await his trial in prison, leaving the family to auction off their grand mansion on Long Island Sound without him to repay the millions of dollars owed the clients of Walker & Lutrec. Then, just days before the trial, Mrs. Walker, frail and aristocratic, is found wandering the streets of Old Greenwich in the middle of the night wearing a taffeta formal from her high school days.

In a small apartment above Aikens' Drugstore, the Walker children band together. They masquerade unity and well-being; to fight off their "sympathetic" neighbors who now see them as charity cases; and to resist their own odd impulses.

Eric, a medical student, succumbs to his many imagined illnesses. Sarah, still in high school, runs away to New York and a career, she thinks, with a famous ballet company. Eliza, the youngest, follows close on Rebecca's heels every minute.

Rebecca is the "good girl," Yale-bound in the fall but, for now, running the house, paying the bills, vehemently defending her father long after the other Walker children have stopped doing so. Then suddenly, Rebecca, the dependable one, loses control on the day of her father's trial.

THE
MASQUERADE

The Masquerade, Susan Shreve's finest young adult novel, is really the story of Rebecca, the "best all-round," as Eric calls her, who abandons the careful mask of respectable young woman in a critical town. Her unexpected wild jaunts until sunrise with a tough and dangerous young crowd *do* have a purpose. But only when she is able to look beyond the masquerade does she begin to sort out her life.

1

Rebecca Walker's father was arrested at his own house on a Monday afternoon in early April.

Rebecca was making fudge in the kitchen and watched with mild curiosity as Edward Walker walked out the long driveway between two dark-suited men of equal size. They were men without distinction, like men with whom her father regularly did business.

"What's Daddy doing home in the middle of the afternoon?" she asked her older brother, home on spring vacation from medical school in Cambridge.

Eric stood in the window next to Rebecca and watched the car with his father and the two men pull away.

"Well?" Rebecca asked, tasting the fudge.

"I thought you had the flu," Eric said. "We'll all have it if you keep sticking your finger in the fudge."

Rebecca shrugged. Ever since Eric Walker had gone to medical school, he'd discovered a hundred things to die from. Lately, he presumed he had the beginnings of a rare nerve disease. He was afraid of germs and showered twice a day.

"I think Eric's going crazy," Rebecca had said to her father. "Every disease in the medical books he thinks he has."

"We'll be the ones to go crazy," her father had said and laughed. "Eric will be fine."

Rebecca Walker was tall, nearly five feet ten, sturdy but not fat, with solid and distinctive features. She would grow better-looking with time, be called handsome when the looks of prettier girls were fading like inexpensive reproductions. But now, at eighteen, she looked younger in spite of her height, and "pleasing," as Eric said, "though not pretty."

"Pleasing," Rebecca had snapped. "I wouldn't talk if I were you. You look like a plastic skeleton which is not too pleasing."

* * *

"They're coming back," Rebecca said as she watched the car with Edward Walker pull back in the driveway. One of the dark-suited men got out and rang the bell.

"I'll get it," Eric said.

Rebecca watched Eric open the door, speak to the man, go to his father's study and come back with a briefcase. The man took the briefcase, got back in the car and drove away. Rebecca watched all this from the kitchen, absently licking the fudge spoon, filling it with germs.

"Shit," Eric said, coming back in the kitchen.

"Who was that?"

"I don't know his name," Eric said. "We're not on familiar terms."

"So what does he want?"

"Daddy's been arrested," Eric said without drama. He sat down and put his head in his hands as though it hurt.

"I don't believe you," Rebecca said quietly.

"Don't believe me, then," he said.

She watched her older brother carefully. He was twenty-three and too thin. He wore wire-rim glasses with thick lenses. She could never really be sure of the expression in his eyes.

"He wasn't even handcuffed."

"No, Rebecca," Eric said. "They don't expect him to be violent between here and Bridgeport."

"Bridgeport?"

"The Fairfield county jail," Eric said. "Those gentlemen in black are the police."

"You're not kidding me, are you?" she asked, surprised at the steadiness of her own voice, the familiar tone.

"I don't have that kind of imagination," he said and gestured towards the stove. "The chocolate's boiled all over the stove," he said. "I'm not kidding about that, either."

She jumped up and turned off the gas.

"Now you can lick what's all over the stove if you want."

"Shut up." She got a rag and wiped off the stove.

"What did Daddy do?" she asked quietly.

"Embezzled," Eric said.

5

Edward Walker had told his son that morning after breakfast.

"Embezzled?" Eric had asked.

"I've been accused of embezzling," Edward said. "I didn't, of course," he added quickly.

"But you've been arrested."

"This afternoon. I understand they are coming this afternoon," he said, straightening his tie in the bathroom mirror, brushing his hair with the palm of his hand. "They'll come to the house and I'll leave with them."

"Jesus," Eric said.

Edward Walker left for work predictably at eight, and Eric walked to the car with him.

"Of course you can be released immediately on bail until you're tried," Eric said with a slight shrug, hoping this dark information about his father was a temporary inconvenience and embarrassment.

"In this town?" Edward Walker said crossly. "Of course I can, but I'll stay in jail in Bridgeport until I'm tried rather than be around to watch the great pleasure Old Greenwich will have in my misfortune."

* * *

Rebecca poured the rest of the chocolate in the sink.

"Aren't you going to make fudge?" Eric asked.

"No," she said, running cold water on the chocolate. "Do you know what happened?"

"They say Dad stole money from his clients," Eric said. "Lots of it. A fortune." He threw his arms open

6

in a gesture to include the kitchen, the library, the whole house. "To buy us all of this."

"But he didn't."

"They say he did," Eric said. "He's been accused and arrested. That's all I know."

"It's a mistake," Rebecca said. She rinsed out the fudge pot and put it away.

"For god's sake, don't cry," he said.

"I'm not," she said.

"You are. I can tell. Your shoulders are shaking."

"I'm not," she said. She turned around so he could see her face. She wasn't crying.

"The thing is, Bec, I think I'm getting this illness I told you about last night."

"Which one?"

"The nerve one. Crying really gets to me."

"Okay," she said. "I'm not crying."

"I know," he said. "I'm sorry to be like this."

He put his elbows on the table and held out his hands. "See?" he said triumphantly. His hands were shaking like flags in the wind.

"Jesus, Eric," Rebecca said. "Maybe you ought to be a lawyer instead."

* * *

Sarah was in her room practicing dance in front of the mirror. She stood with her head at an angle to her shoulders, her body to the side, making bird wings of her arms in the mirror. She had her hair pulled back in a doughnut and bright purple on her cheeks, matching purple on her nails. The room smelled

7

sharply of nail polish and sweet perfume.

"I know," she said to Rebecca without breaking her position. "Eric told me."

"About Dad?"

"Of course," Sarah said. "He said it was *nothing* to worry about."

She bent straight down and touched her lips to her knees. "That it was a matter of form and Daddy'd be released right away." She kicked her leg up to the top of the bedpost. Pointed her toes.

"Eric didn't say that to me," Rebecca said. "How long is right away?"

"Dunno," she said, arching her back and turning very slowly so that her back was to the mirror. "A couple of hours or days. Really short," she said. "You worry so much. Even Eric, the supreme worrier, says so."

"Did Eric tell you he has a nerve disease and dry skin and cancer of the pancreas? Incurable."

"He thinks he has everything," Sarah said, turned twice and sat down on folded legs without stirring the air. She had prizes for dancing and gymnastics in six counties. She dreamed of being famous.

"Anyway," she said, facing Rebecca for the first time. "We've got to believe things are perfectly fine for Eliza and Mother's sake." She stretched her arms in front of her and turned them back and forth like silk flowers.

At sixteen, Sarah Walker was unacquainted with grief.

"When did Mother find out?" Rebecca asked Sarah.

"A few days ago," Sarah said. She was lying on her bed now with the telephone on her stomach. "Daddy told her when he thought he'd been caught, but she didn't tell us."

"Not caught," Rebecca said. "He didn't do anything to be caught for."

Sarah raised her eyebrows.

"Well?"

"Who knows." Sarah said.

"Have you talked to Mother about it?" Rebecca asked.

"Mother told me what she knew this morning."

"She knows he's innocent, doesn't she," Rebecca insisted.

"I don't want to talk about that," Sarah said. "Mother told me he was going to jail." She took the receiver off the hook and dialed. "She was brave about it."

*　*　*

Alicia Walker had come to Sarah's room after breakfast and told her matter-of-factly about Edward Walker.

"Do you think he did it?" Sarah asked her mother.

"I don't know," Alicia said, twisting the hem of her thin spring skirt in her fingers. She could talk to Sarah in a way she would never talk to her older daughter, Rebecca, on whom she depended. Rebecca made her mother feel inadequate, not by design but simply by her own sufficiency.

"I feel terrible about this," Alicia said to Sarah. "As though I'm somehow to blame."

"To blame for what?" Sarah asked.

9

"If . . ." Alicia began. "Let's say he did take money from clients, though I don't think he did. I can't imagine." She put her head back on Sarah's headboard and closed her eyes. "But if he did, it was for me. To make me happy. To buy me all this." She gestured towards the long lawn that rolled down like yards of dark silk to the Sound. "Isn't it silly how backwards everything is?" she said.

"But he didn't embezzle," Sarah said.

"No, of course not," Alicia said. "Anyway, we have to go on and believe that he is right." She embraced her daughter, kissed her on the forehead. "When I was young I wanted to be a dancer too," she said. "Did I ever tell you that?"

*　*　*

In the bathroom, Rebecca pulled the curtains at the window overlooking the Halleys' house so the Halleys couldn't see her crying in case they were looking. She turned on the water in the sink, both spigots hard, so Sarah, in the next room, couldn't hear her.

Then she sat on the floor, rested her head in her arms on the toilet seat, and wept.

Once when she was a child, in the middle of the night, her father had found her in the same bathroom sleeping with her head on the toilet seat—only the rug had been a panda shape then, done over wall-to-wall in raspberry when the girls grew up. He had carried her back to bed.

"I thought I was going to be sick," she'd said. "Can I sleep with you and Mommy?" she'd asked. "I may be sick again," she warned. "Can you stay with me a minute and scratch my back?" And he had stayed, had fallen asleep scratching her back. When she woke in the morning he was half sitting against the headboard and she was sleeping on his chest.

*   *   *

"What are you doing?" Sarah shouted, banging on the door. "Trying to drown?"

"Washing," Rebecca lied.

"I've been calling you to the phone for hours."

"I don't want to talk," Rebecca said. "I'll call back."

"It's Molly. She says it's important."

"You heard me," Rebecca said. "Later."

She checked the mirror over the washbasin and was surprised to see that she looked exactly as she'd always looked to herself in that mirror. Except, close up, especially in the eyes and forehead, the way her hair fell—she blocked out the rest of her face for emphasis—close up, she looked very much like her father.

*   *   *

"I know about Daddy," Eliza said to Rebecca as she came in the room.

"What do you know?"

"He's going to jail for nothing," she said.

"That's right."

"It'll be in the paper," Eliza said. "Eric said there might be a picture on the front page. He said the whole family might be in it."

Rebecca felt ill. She had not thought about the newspapers.

"Is Mother in her room?" she asked Eliza.

Eliza nodded. "She's polishing," she said.

"Polishing?"

"Yup."

Eliza seemed to Rebecca older than seven. Older than Sarah. She seemed intuitively to understand things the other children didn't know.

* * *

Alicia Walker was polishing the things on her husband's dresser—the silver hairbrush and picture frame with a picture of all the children the year Eliza was born, the mirrored dresser top doubling the blue flowered patterns of the room, the gentle face of Alicia Walker.

"Hello," Rebecca said, sitting on the edge of her parents' bed.

Usually the Walkers' bedroom was out of bounds. Alicia Walker maintained a quiet privacy in her own life that belonged to an older generation, remote beyond the lives of Rebecca's grandparents. The children were not certain of their mother's thoughts or if things mattered to her in a large way.

"It's important for girls to learn how to sew," she'd say, or "I believe that ballet lessons teach grace and every girl should take them for a short time," or "I wish I had learned to type so I could have some kind of job," but she spoke in general terms, as though all girls were similar. She never mentioned her daughters in particular ways. Her children didn't tell her about things that mattered to them, and she seldom spoke of things substantial except to Sarah.

It wasn't that the Walker children were afraid of what Alicia would think of them if they told her their secrets, but rather that they were afraid of what might happen to her if she knew, for example, that Rebecca crashed her bike into a street light driving in the dark or that Sarah drank vodka at Missy Clover's and threw up all night or that Eric was living in Cambridge with a woman medical student from Pakistan. Alicia Walker was made of more fragile material than other mothers the Walker children knew. Like a fine china cup with slender edges. They protected her from information that might break her.

"What are you doing?" Rebecca asked her mother.

"Straightening," Alicia Walker said, blankly. "And polishing."

She took Edward Walker's shirts out of the closet and folded them carefully, lining up the sleeves, folding so the corners matched each to each, and put them in the drawer as if they were infants with a life of their own.

"Do you want me to make supper?" Rebecca asked.

"I have chicken out," her mother answered indirectly. "And Eliza needs to go to piano at four. Sarah can walk to dancing." She wandered. "Is Eric home for dinner?"

"I'll ask."

"I'm going to the Crowleys'," she said. "It would be nice if you did dinner, Rebecca. I'll need to finish here."

The room needing finishing was immaculate. Even

13

the tie-back curtains and the quilted spread were newly laundered. The mirrors and the things on the tops of tables shone like polished stones.

"Will Daddy be gone long?" Rebecca asked.

Her mother smiled absently, as though she hadn't heard her daughter's question. "We can have rice," she said. "And there's fresh spinach."

2

Old Greenwich, Connecticut, was a small New England village, a far outpost of New York City, a commuter town, well-to-do, consciously middle class but less pretentious than other Connecticut towns. It had small clapboard houses painted yellow and autumnal brown with complementary shutters, and winding streets and lanes that led at the far end of town to Long Island Sound. Beyond the village was a lake with ducks and small bridges, rolling green hills thick with crocuses and daffodils in early spring. There were model sailboat races on the lake in May. Everyone rode bikes and went to the local public schools, everyone had a boat, or at least a Sunfish, on the Sound in summer and played tennis and racketball throughout the year.

Alicia Walker was from Old Greenwich. She had grown up in an old farmhouse on Roosevelt Street, the daughter of the local lawyer and certified public accountant who handled the affairs of everyone in town except the transients who had lawyers in New

York. It was not a lucrative business, but it was substantial, and Alicia was a child of generations of Georgian silver tea sets and Queen Anne chairs and Oriental rugs delicately worn. There was a sense of well-being about the house which couldn't come of one generation.

She was a quiet child with a lovely gentle manner who preferred the lives of heroines in the romances she read to her own life. She wanted to be well thought of by her classmates in school, admired, but she was thought of simply as a pretty girl who was pleasant and kind. Forgettable. It was not satisfactory for a young woman with an appetite for high romance, and so she retreated to her books.

Alicia met Edward Walker during her sophomore year in college, when he was in law school. She found him charming and exuberant, full of high-minded ideas and plans. He said he would take her to Paris. They would live on a houseboat in England and then in New York, he'd make money and they'd live in a brownstone overlooking Central Park. Perhaps he'd run for Congress from the 108th, his old district.

When he took over the tiny law office on Main Street after Alicia's father died suddenly in 1960, Alicia wept in secret in her bedroom for days.

"It's the baby," she told Eric, who was four at the time and wondered why suddenly his mother was crying all day. "When I'm pregnant," she said, "I sometimes cry." She cautioned Eric not to tell his father, but he did, anyway.

"Perhaps if we could move out of this house where

I grew up," Alicia said of the house on Roosevelt where they had moved when her father died. "It's too full of memories."

By 1968, Edward Walker was a very rich man, and they sold the house on Roosevelt Street to a family from Washington, D.C., and bought the Clauses' house on the Sound—the first time it had been offered for sale in over one hundred years.

"A regular mansion," Eric told his friends. "It even has its own tennis court."

"Don't show off, Eric," Alicia said. "We're no different than anyone else in this town."

Eric cocked his head and looked at his mother. "Only we live in a mansion on the Sound."

In the mansion on the Sound, Rebecca and Sarah had separate bedrooms and a playroom done in bright yellow with a picture window that overlooked the Sound and opened to a screened-in porch where they often slept in summer and listened to the water's steady slap against the sand, to the occasional late-arriving sailboat swishing across the water like a long skirt, to the foghorns in late spring. Eric lived in a turret with windows in a circle around his bed and a separate staircase from the outside. Since his room was set off from the main house, he was allowed to keep animals there—rabbits and hamsters, pet mice which he bred and whose babies he sold off at ten cents each, a snake, a green-and-orange parrot whom the boys in sixth grade at elementary school taught to say "crap" and "hot shit."

* * *

"I was very disappointed when we came back to Old Greenwich," Alicia confessed one evening at dinner. "I had wanted to go to one of those places you used to tell me about when you were in law school. But," she said, "this is a lovely house. I never knew how peaceful it would be to live on the Sound."

Edward Walker knew it was not the sound of the sea that gave Alicia a sense of peace but the house itself—that it was the most elegant house in town, that people on the street who had not known her before knew her now because she lived there, that people who had known her for years and found her shy, withdrawn, looked at her differently at the A & P, the library, the country club, because she and Edward Walker owned the Clauses' house on the Sound. It made her equal to the romances she read in high school.

"Your mother needs that house," Edward Walker said to Rebecca one afternoon as they biked through all the back streets of Old Greenwich. "She's a fine woman, but she hasn't got the confidence to feel worthwhile without large houses and silver," he said with some bitterness. "Her parents cared for her too well."

"But you love her?" Rebecca asked, always confused by her father's annoyances at Alicia Walker.

"Of course I love her," he snapped. "I want her to have this house. Whatever she needs to feel as good as other people in this town."

They parked their bikes and walked along the beach together.

"When I married your mother I thought she was the loveliest woman I had ever known. I was a poor boy, without manners, from Brooklyn, and she seemed just like those long-haired beauties she reads about in her romances. I wanted to do everything for her." He took Rebecca's hand. "It was foolish. We can't ever do things for the people we love."

They took the high road from the beach back through the woods and watched the sun begin to set on a single tree as though it had caught fire. "I'm glad I can depend on you, Rebec," he said as if he intended for Rebecca to make up for Alicia Walker's failures.

When Rebecca was ten, Alicia Walker was pregnant again. For days she stayed in her room with the door shut. She couldn't eat.

"I can't manage another child," Rebecca heard her mother tell Edward Walker one night.

"She could have an abortion," Rebecca said to Sarah.

"Mother?" Sarah said. "Never."

"Would you?" Rebecca asked.

"I'll never get pregnant," Sarah said absolutely.

"This is a difficult time for your mother," Edward Walker said to Rebecca. "I need your help."

It made Rebecca sick. Often at night she couldn't sleep, her legs and shoulders taut as rubber bands, stretched to the point of snapping, her brain jumping like Mexican beans in a glass bottle, full of tomorrow's test and the tennis match on Saturday and what she'd cook for dinner if Alicia had morning sickness again and what to do about Sarah, who might flunk fourth grade, or so the fourth grade teacher had told Rebecca in absolute confidence on the playground after spring vacation.

"I don't know what I'd do without you," Edward Walker said. "You are an incredible daughter."

So Rebecca worked harder, thought of original projects in math, practiced mornings before breakfast on the backboard. She volunteered as a nurses' aide at Greenwich Hospital. She tutored reading on Wednesday afternoons at the Child Guidance Center. She was pale and had thick black circles under her eyes.

* * *

Alicia Walker, six months pregnant with Eliza, had a mild nervous breakdown in February when Rebecca was in sixth grade.

Sarah found her sitting on the floor of the laundry room, weeping. She saw her out of the corner of her eye and didn't go in, called instead. "Mother," she called, "are you okay?"

"Yes," Alicia answered, but the weeping continued and Sarah checked Eric's room for Eric, who was not there, and sat in the living room, listening to the constant heaves of her mother from the back of the house, and waited for Rebecca to come home from school.

"Mother." She motioned with her head in the direction of the laundry room.

"Mother," Rebecca said gently, going over to her, putting her arms around her shoulders.

"Please," Alicia said. "Get your father."

* * *

On the way to the hospital, Rebecca sat in the back seat.

"I can't handle four children," Alicia said over and over again. "I won't be able to keep this baby. I'll give it up."

She went straight from the floor in the hospital for mental patients to the maternity ward, where Eliza was born. She looked beautiful when she came home with the baby in late May, and Edward hired a woman from Bermuda to keep Eliza. She stayed a year and was followed by a Dutch girl who didn't speak English and then by a young woman from Chile and a series of others, but there was always someone to help Alicia with this new child she was afraid would break her.

"Do everything you can for Mother," Edward Walker told Rebecca shortly after Alicia came home with the new baby.

"Of course I will," Rebecca said. And she did. Year after year.

3

The story about Edward Walker was on the front page of the local newspaper with pictures—one of him playing squash, one picture of Edward in black tie with Alicia at a party, and a third of the house, still called the Clauses' house, taken from a boat on the Sound. The article took for granted that Edward Walker embezzled the money.

It gave a sketch of his background as a boy in Brooklyn who had gone to public schools and worked his way through college as a busboy in a delicatessen in New Haven. It spoke with admiration of Alicia's father, of his generosity in giving Edward Walker the business.

"Granddad didn't give Dad the business," Eric said. "He died. Isn't that right, Mom?" he called to Alicia Walker in the kitchen.

"Of course he died," she called back in her gentle musical voice.

"Jesus." Eric threw up his arms. "Have you noticed Mom lately?"

Rebecca nodded.

22

"Air-headed." He held his stomach. "Did you happen to have the leftover cream pie?"

"Nope," she said.

"I think it was tainted," he said. "Well. They don't mention our names in the newspaper story. Four children, it says. Four anonymous children. Not a word about what color hair we have."

"They're trying to give us a break."

"Terrific. I'm touched once again by the modest gentility of the press." He looked through *The New York Times*. "Bec," he called. "Would you mind trying the rest of the cream pie?"

"To see if it poisons me too?" she said. "I think not."

Eric opened *The Times* on the floor. "Well, we're big time. Third page. OLD GREENWICH LAWYER ACCUSED OF EMBEZZLING SEVERAL MILLION DOLLARS FROM CLIENTS OVER THE PAST TEN YEARS."

"Over the past ten years?" Rebecca said.

The stories in the newspapers made Edward Walker's imprisonment fact. It was not a temporary inconvenience, as all the Walkers had pretended to themselves it would be. For days now, Rebecca had not been able to eat anything but yogurt.

"Did you know that?" Rebecca asked.

"I only know what I read in *The Times*, for chrissake."

"Eric, please." Alicia Walker came in from the kitchen. She had on a blue Chinese silk robe that could have been a dinner dress, only she wore it for a robe. She hadn't been out of it for days.

"Please what?"

"Please read the paper to yourself," she said evenly.

*   *   *

Edward Walker had been in prison three weeks.

"He could be out on bail, you know," Rebecca announced one day at lunch in early May.

"Of course he could," Eric said. "He's chicken."

"To stay in jail. To sit in a cell all day and eat that terrible food. To be humiliated," Rebecca said. "I think he's courageous to stay there."

"To hide there," Sarah said.

"It's a lot harder for him there than it would be here with us," Rebecca said.

"Bullshit," Eric said. "Don't delude yourself, Rebec." But before he finished, Rebecca threw the rest of her glass of milk in the sink and left the kitchen.

"Poor Rebecca," Eric said to Sarah after she'd left. "Full of fairy tales."

*   *   *

Rebecca had gone to prison to visit her father with Alicia. Once with Eric. Sarah didn't want to go. The school psychologist said that Eliza should not. Twice Eric had taken Eliza to Greenwich Memorial Hospital with hives, which the doctors said were in all probability due to nerves. Once Eric had gone himself with a pain in his chest.

Rebecca had driven. Eric lay in the back seat of the station wagon and took deep breaths.

"At least," Rebecca said on the drive home an hour

later, Eric sitting in the front seat, "you haven't had a heart attack before."

"Shut up," Eric said.

There was a visiting room, comfortable though sparsely furnished, in the prison, where they met Edward Walker.

"It's very pleasant," Alicia said the first time they went. "It hasn't got wooden benches."

"It's just like a hospital," Eric said. "They ought to have a chapel where the family can go to pray for the patient's recovery."

Edward Walker didn't look like a patient. He seemed thinner than he had been, but he was a short man of heavy Germanic stock who could afford to be thinner. He was quiet, but that wasn't surprising— though a certain look about his eyes was different, as if he had changed the color cosmetically, and in the artificial light his pupils seemed opaque.

* * *

With Alicia at the prison waiting room, Edward was gentle.

"This will be over soon," he told her. "My lawyers are confident."

"That's good," she said vacantly.

"There seems to be no question about winning the case."

"What about money?" she asked. "I have some left from my father."

"Whatever happens, I'm going to have to pay some of that money back even though I didn't take it."

25

"I don't understand."

"Someone in my office took the money, of course. If they can't find him, I'll have to pay it back."

"Do you think Arch Jones did?" Alicia asked.

"I suspect Arch Jones," Edward said. "Even if I'm found innocent, it will be difficult to find work for a while, after all this publicity."

"How will we live?" Alicia asked.

"We must do everything that's necessary."

"Even the house?"

"That's necessary."

When he kissed Alicia, Rebecca turned her head. It made her enormously sad to see them together. She didn't look at her father when they left. It would be impossible for him if he thought she was crying.

In the car going home Rebecca asked about the house.

"What about it?" Alicia asked.

"What did Daddy mean?" Rebecca asked. "He said that we'd have to do what was necessary with the house."

Alicia hesitated. "Paint it," she said awkwardly, lying and unaccustomed to lying. She didn't know how to do it with grace. "If the painting is necessary."

With Eric, Edward Walker was fatherly and in command. "Your job is medical school," he told him. "I understand from Mother that you go back next week, and that's what you're to do," he said. "Mother will take care of the details at home, and I have an excellent lawyer for the problem here, which should be settled in no time."

"How long is 'no time'?" Eric asked roughly.

"Oh, I don't know." Edward Walker hesitated. "A few months."

"That long?" Rebecca blurted out. "What should I do?"

"About what, Rebecca?" Edward Walker asked, as though it was perfectly ordinary in middle-class families to run things from prison.

"About college."

"When you hear," he said, "you should accept whichever college you choose to go to."

"Yale," she said. "If I get in. Can we afford it?"

"Of course," Edward Walker said abruptly, "and if not, there's a delicatessen where I worked my way through Yale." He attempted humor. "You may have read about that in the paper."

Rebecca knew it was folly to think the Walkers could afford Yale when Edward Walker might have to repay millions to people in Old Greenwich, but she dismissed it. When she was small, before her father made money, she used to visit F.A.O. Schwartz at Christmas and pretend that all the toys were hers, and so now she pretended that Yale was hers as well.

As they left, Edward Walker gave Rebecca a note, which she opened in the car and read.

Rebec— I know you will take care of everything while I'm away, but please take special time with your mother and don't fight with Sarah. Love, D.

She folded the letter and stuffed it under her sweater.

"He was just the same," Rebecca said. "Don't you think?"

Eric shrugged.

"Well," she said, "what do you think?"

"Not much," he said. "I've had a headache for ten days," he said. "I can't think. And what little I can leads me to the conclusion that he screwed things up."

"Daddy?"

"Daddy."

The children had been told by their father's lawyer that Arch Jones, a lawyer from New York who was the first man that Edward Walker had hired as a CPA specializing in taxes, had embezzled the money. It made perfect sense. Easily Arch Jones could have done it. He didn't even live in Old Greenwich, lived halfway to New Haven, and looked, according to Sarah, who made decisions on the basis of looks, as though he could steal from old women without a second thought.

It was just a matter of time, they had been told, and everything would be cleared up.

"I know for a fact that Daddy didn't embezzle," Rebecca said coolly.

"He may not have," Eric said. "But for a man who worked ten hours a day, he wasn't very careful about his business."

"It was the other man who worked with him."

"He should have known," Eric said. "He should have known what Arch Jones and every other person who worked for him was doing. This shouldn't have happened."

"He worked harder than anyone I know."

"Don't raise your voice."

"You wouldn't be in medical school."

"Listen, Rebecca, I have a terrible headache," Eric said.

"Good," Rebecca said, slamming the car door, going in the house through the kitchen.

* * *

Rebecca passed Sarah lying on her stomach across the bed, talking on the phone.

"Sarah," she said, propping herself up against the doorway.

"Yeah." Sarah put her hand over the receiver.

"I have to say something."

"Say it."

"Private."

Sarah rolled her eyes, turned over on her back, lifted her legs at right angles with her torso. Pointed her toes.

"Now," Rebecca said.

"I'll call you back," Sarah said to the person on the other end of the line, and slow as a dancer in demonstration she hung up the phone. "So what's private?"

"Why won't you go to prison to see Daddy?"

"Because he'll be out soon."

"He won't be out soon," Rebecca snapped. "He said today it may be months."

"Months?" Sarah sat up in bed and crossed her legs. "Eric said anytime."

"Eric was wrong."

"Well." She got up, went over to the closet and opened it, examining the contents from the doorway. Then she bent down, swinging the top half of her body back and forth like a pendulum across her legs.

"Jesus," Rebecca said. "You drive me crazy."

Occasionally Rebecca had waking dreams of tearing Sarah limb from limb as though she were a mannequin, a leotarded arm here, a leg in black tights there. She dreamed of cutting off the knot of long hair pinned to the back of her head so the uncut hair would stand out like bristles and the rest Rebecca would throw over the sun-porch railing into the rose garden.

"You should go see him," Rebecca said, "but that, of course, is your business."

Later, while Rebecca was lying on her bed reading, Sarah came in, dressed in corduroys, her hair tied back in a ribbon, looking like a regular sophomore in high school. She seemed accessible to Rebecca for the first time in months.

"The reason why I haven't gone to see Daddy," she said quietly, "is that he doesn't want to see me."

"He does. He even wrote me a note about you."

"What did it say?" she asked.

"For me not to fight with you."

"That's for your sake," Sarah said. "Or Mom's. Everything Dad says is for your sake," she said. "Or Mom's."

Half sleeping in the early dusk, Rebecca remembered an Easter years ago, after the egg hunt and church and Easter dinner with Aunt Josephine.

Edward Walker had said, "Rebecca and I are going for a bike ride." And he'd grabbed her up under his arms and swung her around. "Get changed to jeans," he said.

"Can I come?" Sarah had asked.

"Sometime, Sar," he said. "When you're older and get a bike."

"I am older," Sarah said. "I'm eight and got a bike for my birthday," she said. "And Rebecca's been going with you since she was five."

"Sometime soon, then, Sarah," he'd said. "Not today."

Alicia had stopped him when he was going out with Rebecca. "Please," she asked him. "Let Sarah go with you this once."

But when he asked, Sarah said no, she wouldn't go, and turned up the music to the *Nutcracker* as loud as it would play.

She never asked to go again and Edward never took her.

* * *

Later that night when Sarah came home, Rebecca went in her room. She had the furniture pulled back and was practicing gymnastics—handsprings across the bedroom floor. She didn't break time when Rebecca came in.

"I'm sorry," Rebecca said.

"About what?"

"You were right about Daddy."

But Sarah was counting "one-two-three, one-two-three," timing her handsprings, safe behind the discipline of her body.

* * *

When Alicia Walker announced about the house, Eliza was spending the night out.

"I wanted to wait until Eliza was out," Alicia said over dinner, "to tell you about the house."

"I know about the house," Eric said. "We have to sell it. Every goddamned person in Old Greenwich knows but us."

"It's going to be auctioned a week from Saturday," Alicia said. "We have a professional auctioneer," she added, as though that would appease them.

"Why?" Sarah asked.

"We have to do what's necessary," Alicia said, repeating what she'd heard from Edward Walker. "And it's necessary to sell everything to begin to pay back the debt and to have something to live on."

"But we don't owe it," Rebecca insisted.

"It will be proved that he didn't embezzle. But for the moment, he's considered guilty. Even if he's innocent, his firm must repay the debts, and Daddy's head of the firm. Meanwhile," she said woodenly, "we have to do everything that's necessary."

" 'Everything'?" Eric asked suspiciously. "What do you mean 'everything'?"

"Oh, you know." Alicia swung her hand vacantly about the room. "We need to make as much money as we possibly can."

"You mean the furniture?" he asked.

"Not your clothes," she said in defense. "Or Liza's

32

toys. We can each keep a bed and a dresser and a mirror." And then she added impulsively, as though this compensation would mean everything, "We can each choose one special thing. Like the old rocker in my bedroom."

"Jeez." Sarah stormed from the table.

"Where are we going to live?" Rebecca asked, but Alicia only smiled at her and got up from the table, clearing her place and Sarah's, as though she had reached her capacity for loss and closed off all further valves of her being to prevent seepage.

"Terrific," Eric said, looking at Rebecca across the table. "So what did I tell you?"

"About what?"

"About Dad."

She got up from the table without answering.

"Obviously he was responsible, whether he embezzled or not."

In the kitchen, Rebecca loaded the dishwasher. Eric followed her there.

"Aren't you going out with Susan Folles tonight?" she asked, hoping he would leave her alone.

"Edward Walker Associates owes Mr. Folles, amongst others, twenty-five thousand dollars."

"I'm sure she understands that it isn't Daddy's fault."

"Susan doesn't."

"Well, my friends do," Rebecca said.

"Open your eyes," Eric said.

"About what?"

"About what people think now Dad's in jail."

"The same as ever," Rebecca said. "Pretty much."

"Bullshit," Eric said, and then he took a glass pitcher and threw it against the kitchen wall. "That's one less pitcher sold from the personal effects of Edward H. Walker." He sat down at the kitchen table and buried his head in his hands.

In her bedroom, Alicia Walker was packing. She had Edward's clothes folded neatly in one suitcase and her own in another.

"Rebecca," she called as she heard her daughter come up the back steps. "I'm keeping the furniture in the den for our new living room," she said, "because it will bring the least money at auction."

"Why can't we wait to sell our things, Mother?"

"We can't," Alicia said. "Daddy says we can't," she said. "Things, after all, aren't so important," she added without conviction, "but there are a few pieces I want to keep from the house where I grew up. This rocker . . ."

It was an old cherry rocker with an upholstered seat and back.

"What do you think?"

"About the rocker?" Rebecca asked.

Alicia was pensive, fingering the brocade on the back of the rocker. "It should bring a lot," she said. "It's an historical piece from Alexander Hamilton's house." She sat down in the rocker. "I just can't decide. My mother used it with me when I was born, and I used it"—she smiled at Rebecca—"with you and Eric and Sarah and Liza. Did you know I had a child before you and Eric? A little boy named Jonathan who

34

died when he was four days old. We named him. Even a middle name. Jonathan Lutrec. We buried him. It was the only decent thing to do, after all. He did live four days." She got up and smoothed the rocker where she'd been sitting. "It could bring as much as one thousand, I expect. That's a lot of money."

Later in the kitchen Rebecca asked Eric about the child Jonathan, born before them.

"I can't imagine that she's never told us."

"It's not true."

"But she said."

"She had a brother Jonathan who died before she was born and is buried near here."

"Now I remember."

Rebecca picked up the pieces of glass from the broken pitcher.

"Mother must be worse than she seems," she said.

Eric knelt down beside her and picked up the rest of the glass. Together they finished the kitchen and swept the floor, put out the trash and went up to their rooms. It was only nine o'clock.

"Good night," Rebecca said.

Eric ruffled her hair. "Good night, Rebec," he said.

4

The house itself was to be auctioned at four o'clock, but the auction of furniture began at ten, and by eight-thirty people had arrived on bicycles, in cars, on foot, and were milling through the yard, behind the house, in the rose garden.

Alicia had laid out a navy suit and blouse with a soft bow. She secured her hair in a knot at the nape of her neck.

"It's important," she had said the evening before, "to look as well as we can."

"We should look normal," Eric said.

"I'm wearing pants," Sarah said.

"I hate dresses," Eliza said.

But Alicia won. Everyone wore dresses, including Eliza, and Eric wore a suit.

"It's like a celebration," Sarah said, packing her things.

Patty Miller came over with cinnamon buns and coffee.

"Oh, 'Licia," she said to her childhood friend, patting Alicia Walker's arm nervously. "It's terrible," she said. "I feel awful about it."

"Some solace," Eric said, "for Patty Miller to sob in our living room."

Patty had arranged for the apartment over Aikens' Drugs, where the Walkers were moving after the house on the Sound was sold, and someone, probably Patty, paid the first three months rent.

"You'd think we were charity cases," Sarah said.

"We are," Rebecca replied.

"Temporarily."

"Don't kid yourself," Eric said to Sarah. "Dad has to pay this money back whether or not he's the one who took it. Unless they find an employee who did." He gave Sarah a playful punch. "We're poor all right. Candidates for welfare. Numbers four-eight-two to four-eight-seven on the dole lists."

Patty Miller even suggested taking the children to live in her house.

"I'd rather rot in hell than live with Patty Miller and her twins," Sarah said loud enough for Patty Miller, two rooms away, to hear her.

"At least Liza," Patty suggested carefully, sensitive to opposition. Alicia was hesitant. "She could play with the twins. They'd love it."

Eric doubted that the twins, boys eight years old with a solid reputation for bad behavior and impudence at school, would love anything better than tantalizing Eliza Walker.

"It might be best for Eliza, though," Alicia said

37

later to Eric and Rebecca. "Just to be away until the trial."

"No," Rebecca said. "Eliza will stay with us." And Alicia acquiesced.

Eric and Rebecca sat against an old oak where Eliza's wooden swing had been hung so that she could, at the height of the swing's run, see the Sound beneath her.

"I'm not sure how I feel," Eric said. "Whether this is a terrible moment or not."

"It's a terrible moment," Rebecca said fiercely. "It's as though we're being sold off piece by piece, an arm to Mrs. Miller, a fingernail to the Archibald Smiths."

"Don't," Eric said.

"I won't cry."

"We're still the same," Eric said. "We'll go to the apartment on Main Street the same people we are here."

"Not quite." Rebecca moved closer to Eric so their shoulders touched each other.

"I understand why Dad chose to stay in jail," Eric said. "I would have."

"How come?"

"We may be the same, but not him. Whether he bought or stole this stuff we're selling today, it adds up to the hours of his life for twenty years."

"He didn't steal," Rebecca said, and she was crying now.

"Maybe not," Eric said. "Maybe it's all a mistake.

But it would take more courage than he has to be here today with us."

Carefully, so that Patty Miller and her husband, Charles, who were standing next to them, didn't see, Rebecca stepped on Eric's foot, hard with her clogs, until he winced.

"The truth, Rebec," Eric said. "For an honest woman, you have a terrible time with the truth."

* * *

In her bedroom, Eliza sat at her desk drawing pictures of flowers, pansies with intricate black centers. Daffodils.

"Did you see outside?" she asked Rebecca when she came in.

"Hundreds of people."

"I hate them," Liza said matter-of-factly. "I think it's stupid Mother made us dress up for them," she said. Eliza wrote "I hate you" on the paper with pansies and daffodils. She pinned it on the bulletin board. "Are they coming in this room?" she asked.

"Yes," Rebecca said, falling back on the bed. "They'll come in, walk around, mark down what they want and the number of it, and then the bidding will start at noon."

"Well," Eliza said, "whoever buys my bulletin board will know exactly how we feel about them."

In the children's bathroom, Eric erased "fuck you," which Sarah had written in coral-red lipstick.

Sarah sat in the window looking out over the tennis court. She was dressed in a red knit dress and clogs.

Her hair was down, and to Rebecca she looked smaller than usual when she came in her room to borrow a brush.

"You look nice," Rebecca said.

Sarah didn't answer.

"What special did you choose to take?" she asked.

Sarah shook her head.

"Nothing?"

"Nope," Sarah said.

"I took the batik in my room of the girl with birds."

Sarah had not changed position.

"Sarah?" Rebecca went over beside her and Sarah was crying. She put her hand on Sarah's shoulders.

"Don't touch me," Sarah said, shaking her shoulders free.

The children waited together at a small pond in an open field behind the house when the doors opened at ten and the people flooded the house. They waited there until the auctioning began, coming back at noon with sandwiches packed by Eric that morning, sitting unobtrusively on the ground beneath the auctioneer.

"I want to see who gets my canopy bed," Eliza said.

The rest of the children were silent.

The Joneses from next door bought all the dining room furniture, including the highboy, for two thousand dollars, and the Baretis from the house next to the high school bought the Georgian silver tea set which sat on the tea caddy, and the tea caddy went to the Presbyterian minister's wife—that and the guest bedroom, complete including the painting over the bureau and the pewter sconces.

Someone paid twenty dollars for Sarah's ballet barre.

"I thought you'd keep that," Eric said. "What did you keep?"

"Nothing," Sarah said. "My bed and a dresser, like Mother said. "Anyway," she said, "I don't need a barre any longer."

Patty Miller didn't buy a thing. "I simply can't," she said. "It would be such a betrayal of Alicia."

"I recommend that we kidnap Patty Miller and sell her on the black market," Eric said. "Or drown her in the Sound on a dark night."

"She's trying to help," Rebecca said.

"Bullshit," Eric replied. "She's having a wonderful time."

* * *

From time to time, Alicia Walker came out on the front porch and wandered behind the auctioneer, looking into the crowd.

She was clearing up last-minute details, she said. The children should remember who bought what and everything that happened for her.

She was standing in the door on the front porch when Alexander Hamilton's rocker came up. In the early afternoon sun, she looked younger than forty-five, without defenses.

"It's Mother's rocker," Rebecca said.

* * *

The children had decorated the nursery when Alicia came home from the hospital with Eliza. They had stretched yellow crepe paper and white rosettes across the ceiling, filled the room with flowers—daisies and white roses from the garden, purple lilacs just in bloom, filling the room with the promise of summer.

ELIZA HOLBROOK WALKER, Sarah had written on a sign. MAY 26, 1970. 6 LBS. 8 OZS.

Rebecca had re-covered the cherry rocker herself in an oriental print of perfectly made branches with white flowers like dogwood against a rich background the color of earth. The old upholstery was tattered from years of children, worn on the seat, faded from the sun on the back of the chair. Rebecca worked for nights after school so the chair would be ready when Alicia came home from the hospital with this late baby, this unexpected daughter. Edward Walker brought champagne, and in the late afternoon of Memorial Day brought home his wife, who had been gone three months, and his last-born child. That evening the Walker family sat in darkness, warmed by champagne, listening to the familiar creak of the old rocker and to the sounds of Eliza Walker, exploring her sweet new world.

* * *

"I'm asking fifty for this rocker," the auctioneer said. "Anybody give me fifty?"

There was no response.

"This rocker is worth a fortune," he chided. "Ladies and gentlemen, fifty?"

A hand went up.

"Seventy-five," he said. "Come on now. Seventy-five dollars for a rocker two hundred years old that came from Alexander Hamilton's house."

* * *

The rocker went for one hundred and fifty to strangers. Rebecca watched her mother shrink from the door and go in the house.

"I'll be back," she whispered and jumped up the steps, went into the house. Her eyes burned. She was afraid that when she found her mother, she wouldn't be able to speak.

Alicia Walker sat in a straight-back chair in the dining room, which belonged now to the Spencer Joneses. She was not crying. But in her hand she twisted a linen handkerchief in a long roll and she looked in her elegant distance as though she was preserved from a past century.

"I saw about the rocker," Rebecca said. "That's shitty."

"You should watch your language, Rebecca," Alicia said automatically. She got up and went to the bay window overlooking the rose garden. "I shouldn't have expected a price for that rocker," she said. "It's irreplaceable."

* * *

In the bathroom, Rebecca took out the note her father had given her in prison the week before. It was wrinkled from reading and reading. She read it again, weeping freely behind the closed doors, the voice of the auctioneer barely audible from the front door, her mother's low heels tapping back and forth from the kitchen to the hall and back again as though she was busy with something important—as all of the personal effects of Edward Walker were divided up among the

43

people of Old Greenwich and Darien and Cos Cob. As though it were the man himself divided and portioned out. In this last week, Rebecca felt entirely responsible for her father's reputation. Even Eric had given up.

Eric found Rebecca in the bathroom putting on makeup—foundation and rouge, loose powder, lines under her eyes, doing tricks from her mother's makeup case.

"Makeup?" he said. "I don't think I've ever seen you wear makeup," he said.

"It's to cover up," she said, and in the mirror he could see that her eyes were red and swollen from crying. "To show all the wonderful people out there that the Walker children are perfectly fine without a thing. They can buy it all and take it home," she said.

She took the end of the lipstick tube and drew a clover in strawberry on her cheek.

"A masquerade," she said. "The children's masquerade."

* * *

The house was sold by four-thirty to a family named Farmer who lived on Lincoln Avenue and who had four children just the age the Walker children had been when they had moved into the Clauses' house.

By nine, the few remaining possessions had been moved into the two-bedroom apartment above Aikens' Drugs where Mrs. Aikens, who inherited the store from her husband, had lived until she died.

"You see," Alicia said, standing in the window of the living room of the new apartment, "we'll be able to see everything that happens in town from here. Right now I see Elsa Baker, who bought your father's desk, coming out of Jensen's with a begonia basket."

"Terrific," Eric said, sprawled out on the couch. "What a terrific opportunity."

5

The apartment over Aikens' Drugstore had two bedrooms in the back of the building overlooking the alley where deliveries were made to the shops along Main Street.

"Wonderful," Eric said. "We can get up in the morning to the sweet sounds of the A & P meat truck."

Rebecca and Sarah shared the bedroom papered in fat pastel flowers.

"Like funeral bouquets," Sarah said, arranging her clothes in the dresser.

"We could paint the room yellow," Rebecca said.

"Paint costs money," Sarah said, narrowing her eyes at Rebecca as though her sister were responsible for their financial situation.

"So does food," Rebecca snapped back. "We don't plan to stop eating."

"We're going to steal it," Eric shouted from the living room, "in keeping with the family tradition."

The plan was that Eric would sleep on the couch in the living room when he was home from medical school and that Eliza would sleep with her mother in the lavender-striped bedroom, where, according to the girl at the prescription counter, Mrs. Aikens had been found dead, bloated as a raft, two days after she had actually died.

In the middle of the first night in the new apartment, Eliza climbed into bed with Rebecca.

"I can't sleep," she whispered. Rebecca moved over to make room.

"Bad dreams?" she asked.

"Nope," Eliza said. "Mother."

The next morning, she told Rebecca that she thought she'd move her bed into the pastel-flowered room.

"Mother wants to sleep by herself," Eliza said evasively.

"You know, Rebecca," Alicia said later while Rebecca was helping her scrub the kitchen cabinets, "it will be better if Liza sleeps with you. I like to stay up late."

"So does Sarah," Rebecca said. "Practicing her stupid bends until midnight."

"I still think it would . . ." Alicia began but forgot to finish her sentence, concentrating instead on the careful arrangement of teacups and saucers on the cabinet shelves.

"Was Mother crying?" Rebecca asked Eliza later. "Is that why you couldn't sleep?"

"Not exactly," Eliza said.

They had moved Eliza's bed into the flowered room and were unpacking her stuffed animals.

47

"She seemed funny, that's all," Eliza said.

"What do you mean 'funny'?"

"I woke up in the middle of the night because the light was still on," Eliza said, "and Mother was putting on makeup." She shrugged. "You know, blue paint on her eyelids."

*   *   *

Eric was lying on his stomach in the living room when Rebecca went in to tell him Eliza's story.

"You've got to admit it's very strange to be putting on makeup in the middle of the night," she said.

"Listen, Rebecca," Eric said, hugging the couch cushion. "There's not one normal thing in this family that I can presently see."

"I'm normal," Rebecca said. "Perfectly normal in comparison."

*   *   *

On Main Street, she watched Johnny Barber come out of the A & P with a load of groceries. They had been good friends for years. Last February, before the trouble, he'd asked her to go skiing with him, and she'd said no without a reasonable excuse because she sensed that he was interested in her romantically.

"There's Johnny Barber," she said.

"I have stomach cramps, Rebecca, and I'm trying to get some sleep." Eric rolled off the couch onto his back, taking one cushion with him, holding it over his face. "I want to die," he groaned.

"I hope you get your wish," Rebecca said, stepping on the pillow over his face.

*   *   *

Rebecca Walker didn't have close friends. She was well liked, respected by many groups, one of the few young women at Old Greenwich High School whom it was safe to tell your secrets to, but she maintained a personal privacy, an external sense of well-being that did not seem to require the understanding of friends.

"Best all-around," as Eric said. "Just a regular, ordinary all-around girl." Which was the reputation that Rebecca had, although Eric knew that it was a false one.

* * *

Rebecca watched her mother arrange the kitchen. Alicia was wearing the Chinese kimona she had been wearing for weeks, and makeup was smeared slightly around her eyes. Her hair fell around her face like a nun's habit and she smiled to herself. Not smiled, exactly, but she had a quiet smirk, as if in disapproval of the drama now playing in her mind.

"Do you feel okay, Mother?" Rebecca asked.

"Take vitamins," her mother said absently. "If you want to stay healthy, take vitamins." She looked at Rebecca directly. "I'm going to get a job," she said.

"What kind of job?" Rebecca asked, annoyed at her mother for the first time, out of sympathy with this gentle woman who never raised her voice, who wept in private.

"Why, a perfectly ordinary job, darling, like everyone else." She sat down at the kitchen table and smiled at Rebecca, a cockeyed smile so that her lips curled up her cheeks like vines. In spite of herself, in spite of every control, Rebecca said sharply, "You'll have to behave like a perfectly ordinary woman if you're going to get an ordinary job."

Rebecca got up and slammed the door to the pastel-flowered room, sat with her back to Sarah, who was removing purple polish from her toenails, and to Eliza, who stood in the window watching the surgical supply truck unload.

Alicia Walker had been a storybook mother when Rebecca was small, lovely and quiet with a soft voice and gentle manner, as though she had been made up for a theatrical performance of the perfect mother. She had been an only daughter born late in her parents' lives, raised in a nineteenth-century manner, as though she were only partially human and ill suited to a world larger than the streets that led to Old Greenwich from the small frame house where she lived all of her life. Her mother, for fear of losing this one late baby, promised Alicia Walker that the world beyond Old Greenwich was full of danger, and her father, who had been carefully trained by generations of men to protect the women they loved, would not allow Alicia to work, but sent her instead to lessons in the summer and then to Connecticut College, which was an all-women's school then and was an hour and a half trip by car from Old Greenwich. If her parents were displeased with her choice of Edward Walker when she was nineteen, they showed it only by insisting that he be prepared to take over the Lutrec accounting firm, the family business, in the event of an emergency.

The Walker children knew their mother was fragile and were protective of her, as though she were blind and needed to be led through unfamiliar territory. They also knew that she had a special beauty, like a rare wild bird, which set her apart from other mothers.

"Like a princess," Eliza said about Alicia Walker. And once in anger, Edward Walker had shouted so the children could hear: "You're so distant, Alicia—as though you were born with royal blood."

* * *

"Has anybody asked you out since this all started?" Rebecca asked Sarah.

"I don't have time," Sarah said.

"I didn't ask about time," Rebecca said. "I was just thinking about Johnny Barber. In February, he asked me to go skiing."

"The boys in my class like sports and sex," Sarah said, dressing for ballet class. "Sex and sports. They're boring." She put her hair in a bun. "I don't even like boys."

"Including Eric?"

"Most of all Eric."

"Well, at the moment I like Johnny Barber, but I'm beginning to think Eric's right," Rebecca said. "People do think of us differently. Like the Barbers would probably never consider asking me to go skiing now."

The bathroom had an old tub on feet and no shower.

"I won't bathe," Eric said.

"Eric," Alicia said, "we'll have company. You have to bathe for company."

"Even my apartment in Cambridge has a shower, for chrissake," Eric said.

"You'll have to change at least, Eric," Alicia said. "The Bakers are coming with dinner."

"With dinner." Eric flung the pillow cushion at the couch. "Save the Walkers week. The Dorsets bring dinner and then the Carswells bring groceries and now the Bakers tonight with dinner, for chrissake. They'll bring it in a basket and put it outside the door. What do you want to bet?"

"I just want you to bathe for the company, Eric," Alicia said reasonably.

"What company?" Eric said. "They're not going to come in this place and eat dinner with us. Don't delude yourself, Mother. Old Eedie Baker, Wellesley fifty-five, queen of the country set, champion of mixed doubles and a whiz at bridge, is going to dispense with her Christian duty in a basket outside our door, and I'm supposed to bathe for that?"

"I won't be home for dinner," Sarah said. "I have a long practice."

"What will you eat?" Alicia asked.

"I'll eat later," Sarah said.

"Sarah has decided not to eat at all," Eric said. "She's interested in the aesthetic value of bones."

* * *

At two, Alicia left for a job interview. She wore a simple navy suit and her hair pulled back in a bun.

She had scrubbed off the makeup from the night before.

"Probably I shouldn't dress up," she said to Rebecca. "I need to look responsible and plain," she explained. She had never had a job interview before, she told her eldest daughter. She had never had a job.

"I want you all to work, especially you girls," Alicia Walker had told Rebecca. "My father wouldn't allow me to work, as though working were harmful or I was too weak to do anything."

"You never had a job?" Rebecca asked.

"Never," Alicia said, "and I began to believe my father that I hadn't got the strength for it."

* * *

"Do you know where she has an interview?" Eric asked.

Rebecca shook her head.

"Jeez."

"Sick again?"

"Shut up."

"I wish it were Monday. I want to go back to school. Spring vacation is awful," Rebecca said.

"Is it a full-time job?"

"I don't know," Rebecca said. "It's whatever she can get, I suppose. She's never worked. She's not qualified for anything."

"She's a mother," Eric said. "She's qualified for that."

Rebecca shrugged. The apartment was too small. Eric took up the living room with his anger.

* * *

The phone company came and put a new phone in the kitchen. Eliza called everyone she could think of after it was installed.

"Isn't it wonderful," she said to Rebecca, genuinely pleased. "We have a telephone."

Sarah called to say she was spending the night at a friend's next door to the old house.

"At least we have a phone now," she said to Rebecca.

"How does our house look now?" Rebecca asked.

"Like it belongs to someone else."

"It does," Rebecca said. "Please remember to eat something for dinner."

"One mother is enough," Sarah said.

* * *

Alicia came back at four and said she had a job. Her cheeks were flushed and she smiled an ordinary open smile.

"What kind of job?" Eric asked.

"I have to start out at the bottom," Alicia explained. "You understand I've never had a job."

"What is the bottom?" Eric asked, not kindly.

"I'm going to be working at the checkout counter at Aikens'," Alicia said. "That's where I've been," she said. "Learning to operate the cash register."

* * *

Mrs. Eedie Baker, still in tennis whites, arrived at six with a basket of lasagne casserole and French bread. Eric answered the door.

"Wonderful," he said fiercely. "More charity. Won't you come in?"

"I can't, Eric," she said, handing Eric the basket. "How's your mother?" she asked. "Alicia?"

"Mother's fine," Eric said. "Splendid. I know she'd like to see you. In fact," he said conscious of embarrassing her, "she said you might eat with us. That she was expecting you to."

"I can't," Eedie Baker said, backing out the front door. "There's a cocktail party and I've got to get the kids dinner."

* * *

"Rebecca," Eliza said to her sister, who was dressing, "Mrs. Baker's here with dinner."

"Big deal," Rebecca said.

"You better go 'cause Eric's in a bad mood."

"Eric's always in a bad mood," Rebecca said, but she went out to the living room anyway, just as Mrs. Baker was leaving.

"Mrs. Baker is passing out meals for shut-ins tonight," Eric said to her. "And criminals."

"Eric," Eedie Baker said awkwardly, "I'm surprised at you. I'm sorry," she said to Rebecca. "I was trying to help. I didn't know."

"Know what?" Eric asked. Rebecca went with Mrs. Baker down the steps from their apartment that led out to the street by Aikens' Drugs.

"I apologize for Eric."

"No problem," Mrs. Baker said brightly. "No problem at all." But Rebecca was certain Eedie Baker would have a story for the people at the cocktail party that night.

"He's depressed, of course," she said.

55

"Of course," Mrs. Baker said, anxious to get away.

"Welfare," Eric shouted down the steps at them. "Any handout you've got, Eedie. Old clothes, maybe. Pots and pans. Anything you might have around."

"Jeez, Eric," Rebecca said when she came back upstairs. "Maybe you'd better go back to school right now."

"Maybe so," Eric said, "if things keep up like this."

Alicia sat on the couch in the living room and twisted a handkerchief in her hand.

"I'm sorry," Eric said. "I'm sorry, Mother. I don't mind Eedie Baker, who isn't worth my high blood pressure. What I mind worse than I can say is you working at the cash register at Aikens' Drugs."

* * *

Eric left after midnight. Rebecca heard him packing in the living room and got up.

"I haven't studied for two weeks," he said.

"You didn't tell Mother you were leaving."

"I decided after she went to bed to take the night train to Boston."

"What about Daddy?"

"Listen, Rebecca," he said evenly and without drama, "I hate my father."

* * *

At dawn, Rebecca got up and tiptoed into the living room, half believing, hoping, that Eric had changed his mind, had decided to stay one more week until medical school resumed. But he was gone, and she lay down on the couch where he had spent the first night of their new life, and waited until morning.

6

Rebecca Walker had wanted to go to Yale since she could remember. Since her father bought her a Yale jersey, child's size, which she wore to bed every night for months.

"Following in your father's footsteps," Eric had said. "Like father, like daughter. You might consider grand larceny."

"Shut up," Rebecca had said, at a loss with Eric's anger.

"I can't imagine going to a school with more men than women," Sarah had said, practicing backbends on the living room rug. "With any men, for that matter, given a choice."

"I would be very proud to have a daughter of mine at Yale," said Alicia, who hadn't gone to college and occasionally regretted it, although she was by nature uncomfortable with regret.

* * *

In the winter of her junior year, Edward Walker had taken Rebecca to Yale on the train, just the two of them, escaping the dark February of Old Greenwich. They'd had such a day of it, such a wonderful day full of Edward's stories of Yale while they walked by the places where he had spent four years, that on a lark they'd decided to go out to dinner and they'd missed the last train home.

* * *

"I want to go to Yale for intellectual reasons," Rebecca had argued with Eric. "Not personal."

"Called father worship," Eric said. "Very intellectual."

Rebecca was not the most outstanding student in the class of 1978 at Old Greenwich High, but in all probability she was the most reliable.

"Best all-round," Eric told her always. "In the fifties, when everyone had titles under their graduation picture, you'd have been voted 'Best All-Round' and I'd be 'Most Interesting.'"

"As in 'neurotic,'" Sarah said.

Rebecca was on the honor roll, nominated for every position of leadership although she was seldom elected, chosen by the teachers for responsible positions, a member of the Glee Club and on the newspaper staff, a minor member of the casts of dramatic productions, a good athlete, a team player, always first string.

"Unexceptional," she said glumly to Eric.

"A good wife and mother," Eric said irreverantly to her. "Take heart."

"That's true," Alicia said. "Rebecca holds things

58

together. Look at what she does in our family. Everyone depends on her."

"A veritable earth mother without the breasts," Eric said.

"Jeez, Eric," Sarah said. "I hope you get scurvy in medical school and peel away."

*   *   *

Eric had been the most outstanding student in his class at Old Greenwich, but difficult, with a reputation for arrogance and bad sportsmanship. Sarah was, as her teachers said, "inconsistent," flunking regularly one subject or another, never the same one. For long periods of time she refused to do any homework and fiercely supported such causes as feminism and abortion without involving herself in groups. She was bad-tempered and had few friends. Boys, especially the boys at Old Greenwich High, were afraid of her.

"You'll be a great old maid, Sarah," Eric said. "The terror of Old Greenwich."

"I'm going to be an old maid in New York," Sarah said. "You'll end up in Old Greenwich fixing pimples or taking off corns."

Eliza was by nature good-tempered and lazy, accustomed to Rebecca's resourcefulness, waiting for things to happen, the youngest. Except for her mother's illness when she was very small and unaware and the recent trouble with her father, Eliza, during the years at the Clauses' house on the Sound, had had a quiet and easy life. She was the one sibling loved by all the others, a favored child.

Sarah, like her mother, was lovely in surprising and inappropriate ways, with black hair, high and pointed cheekbones, eyes like olives without warmth. She was too thin and moved with the self-conscious gestures of a dancer. In time, Eliza would resemble her, but would be softer, more awkward and accessible. Unlike the others, Rebecca was undistinguished in a group, favoring her father, who was fair and blue-eyed, with the high color of the English, squarely built, an ordinary man to look at except for the color in his cheeks.

"What does it matter if Sarah's prettier?" Eric asked. "She's also meaner."

"I'm getting too fat," Rebecca said.

"You could cut your hair," Eric said, "and wear eye makeup so you wouldn't be so pale."

But it didn't greatly matter to Rebecca how she looked, at least enough to make changes. Primarily she wanted to please—her father, her teachers, her mother, the world of adults she had been expected to imitate since childhood. Unlike Eric, who was expected to be difficult, or Sarah, who was self-centered, or Eliza, who was the youngest.

"Every family deserves one good girl," Eric said.

* * *

When the thick envelope came from Yale University in the middle of April, Rebecca called her father at prison. The policeman who answered the telephone made arrangements for her to see Edward Walker immediately.

* * *

"I hear you got into Yale," Johnny Barber called, catching up with her after school. "The only one in the class," he said. They walked along Main Street together, by Aikens' Drugs, where Alicia Walker stood at the checkout counter.

"Michael Ryan got in," Rebecca said, conscious of an unexpected shyness. She had known boys as friends, not lovers. She knew that lovers would come in time, later, and she thought often about making love as she tried to get to sleep at night, but always with faceless men, not the boys from Old Greenwich whom she'd known since grade school. Now she memorized the way Johnny Barber's hands moved when he talked, the gray color of his eyes in the sun.

"I'm sorry about skiing in February," she said.

"Yeah, well, that's okay," he said. "I sort of forgot about it."

On impulse he bought her a teddy bear the size of her little finger at Quigley's Gifts.

"To remember me by," he said, "when you go off to Yale."

Just as he turned down Lincoln, where he lived, he asked her to go to the Ottos' party that night if she hadn't been asked already, which she had not been, not asked anyplace since the move, but she didn't tell Johnny Barber that. He said he'd pick her up after dinner at about eight.

* * *

There was a letter from Eric in the mail.

    Dear Rebecca the Good,

        I'm sorry I left like I did and was generally a shit,

61

but a shit I am. I also have double pneumonia and a rare bacteria which attacks the liver, contracted from my Pakistani live-in, named Gayatri. Her liver is more regenerative than mine.

I hope if you do get into college (no chance you won't. Best all-around and all that) you'll go. Meanwhile, worry about Mother, who's in terrible shape. I just don't know what to expect from her. The worst, I guess.

A psychiatrist friend of mine says that boys don't forgive fathers as quickly as girls, which is, I suspect, as much bullshit as most psychiatry. But you may gladly hang onto it if you need to, since forgiving is not first on my list this spring.

And lastly, Rebec, this from the heart and soul of a man whose every other organ is disintegrating with the speed of light—take care of yourself. You're all we got, baby. I've got six months at best.

Love, Eric

* * *

Alicia Walker didn't sleep. Rebecca could hear her moving around the lavender-striped bedroom, occasionally taking a bath in the tub on feet, her light on until morning. Once just after the alarm had gone off at seven, Sarah had found her sleeping on top of the made bed in a long dress, a taffeta formal, rose-colored and with tiny straps and a gathered skirt that snapped when she walked—an old dress from her high school days at Old Greenwich which used to be kept in the dress-up box when Sarah and Rebecca were growing up.

"Christ," Sarah said after she found her mother

and woke Rebecca with a harsh shake of her shoulders.

"Mother." Rebecca woke her gently. Alicia Walker sat up, a puzzled expression on her face, as though Rebecca, her eldest daughter, the caretaker of her house, was unfamiliar in the morning light.

"I must have fallen asleep," she said, standing beside her bed, smoothing the large creases in her dress. Rebecca shut the bedroom door so Eliza wouldn't see them.

Sarah spent the next three nights at a friend's house. When Rebecca called her to find out when she'd be home and if she had passed the history test and didn't she need more clothes, Sarah said sharply, "You can bring over the rose taffeta formal when you have a chance."

* * *

The boys from New Canaan hung around Aikens' Drugstore. That's what Alicia Walker called them: "The boys from New Canaan."

"They are not," she added, "from nice families, as far as I can see."

Occasionally when Rebecca passed, one or another of them would make a smart remark or whistle, and one introduced himself as Billy Thrower and asked if she knew a guy named Handleman on Jackson Street.

"I'd stay away from them," Alicia Walker said. "They're bound to cause trouble."

"I'm not around them," Rebecca said, "except for passing them on the street, which I can't exactly help. It's not a private street."

She did notice them and was even, to her own astonishment, curious about them.

"Because they're different than the people we go to school with," she told Sarah.

"Creeps," Sarah said. "But so are the boys at Old Greenwich."

* * *

Rebecca met her father in a small room with office furniture. He was dressed like a prep-school boy, in brown corduroys and an Irish fisherman's sweater, although it was warm for April. He was tired and seemed ill at ease.

Instinctively she knew it was the wrong moment for good news.

"I was told it was an emergency, that you wanted to come over this afternoon, not at visiting hours," he said with mild irritation. "I thought it might be about Mother."

"Has Mother seemed ill to you?" Rebecca asked.

"Mother has seemed— oh, I don't know." Edward Walker raised his shoulders in question, slouched down in his chair. "Predictable. Fading," he added.

"It's not Mother," she said. She decided not to tell him about the rose taffeta formal, and pulled the letter from Yale out of her pants pocket. "It's this," she said and handed it to him, pleased with the drama of surprise, fixed on his expression. Waiting, expecting the exclamation, which, when it came, was instead a quiet shift of breath, a look which was less disappointment than disinterest. But certainly not pleasure, the absolute pleasure she had expected.

"You're not pleased," she said too quickly.

"It's wonderful, of course," he said.

"We can't afford it," she said. "That's what you mean."

"There are loans," he said, recovering. "Certainly you can go in the fall." He sat up, reached over and touched her hand. "This is fine news."

But Rebecca didn't quite believe him. She hurried through the incidentals of the last week since she'd seen him to be done with this disappointing visit with her father, whom she had expected to save from his own private disappointments with the great news from Yale of his daughter's acceptance.

*   *   *

On the way home that afternoon, she thought about the money for Yale. Surely, if they'd had to sell the Clauses' house and their things, as Alicia referred to them, if Edward Walker had to repay the clients of Lutrec and Walker in spite of his innocence, there would be no money for Yale. But Eric, after all, was in medical school at Harvard.

"Borrowed," Eric told her later. "Doctors are good risks."

"What about women undergraduates at Yale?" she'd asked.

"Who knows, Rebec," he'd said. "You usually end up on your feet."

And in spite of the nagging uncertainty, Rebecca believed that somehow Edward Walker would make arrangements, as he always had.

*   *   *

Sarah came home at eleven and Rebecca was glad to see her because Johnny Barber had not picked her up at eight to go to the Ottos' party.

"Stood up?" Sarah asked. "The bum."

"I guess," Rebecca said.

"Maybe you should try the boys from New Canaan," Sarah said. "Or no one, like me."

"No one sounds better."

7

Sarah left the first day of May, when the daffodils around the pond were in the full bloom of late spring.

Eliza woke Rebecca in the middle of the night to tell her. "Sarah hasn't come home yet," she whispered.

They slept together. They had slept together since the move, and lately Eliza followed Rebecca everywhere, close on her heels, so that one unexpected move could cause a collision between them.

"I know it's after midnight," Eliza said. "I heard Clancy's close."

In fact, it was three o'clock in the morning.

Rebecca got up and put on her robe.

"Call Eric," Eliza said, drawing the covers around her shoulders, pulling her knees up under her chin.

"A terrific idea," Rebecca said. "Unless he's died in his sleep."

"Don't say creepy things," Eliza said. "You could make them happen."

"Shhh," Rebecca said. "You might wake Mother."

"Eric at least will know what to do."

"In emergencies," Rebecca said, "I have more faith in pigeons."

She took Eliza in her arms and they sat together on the bed in darkness, wrapped in blankets, waiting for dawn.

"Sarah probably spent the night at a friend's," Rebecca said, unconvinced.

"She would have called," Eliza said. "Even Sarah would call."

"I suppose," Rebecca said.

They sat up in bed until morning, as though they expected Sarah to come in any moment but were somehow resigned, even before dawn, to the fact that she would not.

"Do you think Daddy stole the money?" Eliza asked once.

"No," Rebecca said. "I've told you no a hundred times."

"Lissy Martin said so," Eliza said. "Her parents told her. She told me nicely," Eliza insisted. "She wasn't trying to be mean."

"If I see Lissy Martin, I'll drown her in a sewer."

* * *

Lately Rebecca had been quick to fight back. One false move from anybody about Edward Walker, one question of his absolute innocence, and she attacked like an alley cat. It had gotten so she could feel changes in her blood, as though the blood itself charged through flimsy inner dams, breaking dangerously inside her. Once Andrew Fortua, the captain of the lacrosse team, well thought of and an old friend, asked Rebecca about her father and did she think he'd get off even if he was found guilty?

"He's fine," she'd snapped. "He's perfectly fine and he'll not be found guilty."

"Listen, Bec," Andy said, "don't be so hot about it. I'm sorry."

And she had a sudden vision of jumping on the back of Andrew Fortua and biting his pink fleshy neck.

"I'm going to pieces," she told Eric on the phone.

"Terrific, Bec," Eric said. "Join the rest of us."

She told him about Andrew Fortua.

"For chrissake, Rebecca, I'd never have suspected it of you," Eric said. "That's wonderful news. Next time, bite him, but not in the back of the neck. He might recover," he said. "Go for the front."

* * *

At dawn before Alicia woke up, Rebecca called Eric in Cambridge. Gayatri answered the phone.

Eric, she said, had stomach flu and couldn't come to the phone.

"I don't care if his stomach fell out during the night," Rebecca said. "I have to talk to him."

"Listen, Rebecca," he said when he came to the phone, "Gayatri's right. I do have stomach flu. There's a high percentage of illness amongst first-year medical students."

"Fatality rate too, I suppose," she said.

"Did you call at this hour to be cute?"

"I called because Sarah's gone."

"Gone?"

"Gone. She had a gymnastics tournament in New Canaan and was due back at nine-thirty. I've already called the Freemonts, who took her, and they said they couldn't find her after the tournament and assumed she'd gone home with someone else, so they left."

"And she probably did go home with someone else."

"I have this funny feeling that she's left."

"I don't know why we all haven't run away."

"We had a fight last night," Rebecca said.

"Have you called the police?"

"Not yet," she said.

"Call them," Eric said, "and the gymnastics coach and the place in New Canaan. And keep it from Mother as long as you possibly can," he said. "And you might, if you go to prison today during visiting hours, tell that prince of a father how grateful we are for tests of inner strength with which he's provided us."

Rebecca hung up.

"I hate Eric," she said to Eliza.

"You don't mean it," Eliza said, hanging on Rebecca's robe, following her into the bathroom. "Just say you don't mean it and I'll leave you alone."

"I hate Eric," Rebecca said slowly. "*Hate*," and she put her arms around Eliza and kissed the top of her head.

"See," Eliza said. "You don't really hate him."

*　*　*

"So you plan to go to Yale," Sarah had said the day before she left home. She had come home early to get ready for the gymnastics tournament, and Rebecca was writing a paper on Flannery O'Connor.

"Yup," Rebecca had answered.

Sarah took a yogurt from the refrigerator and sat down next to Rebecca at the kitchen table.

"From whom are you stealing the money?"

"I'm borrowing it."

"Mmm." Sarah licked the vanilla yogurt slowly off the spoon. "And I stay home with Mother and Eliza."

"I presume," Rebecca said. "Daddy says he may be out right after the trial."

"I'd be just as happy if he stayed in permanently."

"Sarah."

Sarah rested her chin on stacked fists.

"That's true," she said. "What do you want? Fairy tales?"

"It's a terrible way to feel about your father."

"Yes, it is," Sarah agreed coolly. "Did you ever think of going?" She played with the edges of Rebecca's term paper.

"Where?"

"Just going," Sarah said, waving her arms around the room. "Away from here."

"Nope."

"Noble Rebecca," Sarah sighed.

"I don't want to fight."

"You never want to fight."

"Listen, Sarah, it's been bad enough."

"That's what I mean," Sarah said evenly. "It's bad enough that I don't want to stay in this place with Eliza and poor Mother wandering the house in prom dresses."

* * *

Eric arrived on the late-afternoon plane from Boston. He was pale.

"You look like you really had the stomach flu," Rebecca said.

"It could be parasites," he told Rebecca.

"I don't care," Rebecca said, hugging him. "I'm immune to parasites," she said. "I honest to God never in the world thought I'd be so glad to see you."

Eric and Rebecca spent the whole next day with the police in Old Greenwich and then in New Canaan. They spoke with people who had last seen Sarah and with her gymnastics teacher and with Missy Clover, who was glad to supply answers whether they were true or not. The police, especially those in Old Greenwich, were compassionate but neither helpful nor optimistic.

"Runaways," the chief of police said. "They've got us beat. We lose kids all the time, especially in the suburbs. They just drop out like they've never been. Some don't surface for years."

"What do you think?" Rebecca asked Eric on the way home that evening.

"Nothing," Eric said. "Nothing whatever. I've found that thinking, for the most part, interferes with my peace of mind."

*　*　*

Sarah had been gone four days. Missy Clover said she was certain that she'd gone to New York, because she'd talked of running away to New York for weeks.

"Maybe she made it up," Rebecca said. "Missy likes tragedy."

"Let's invite her to move into the apartment," Eric said. "She'll have a blast."

*　*　*

On Saturday, Mr. Clark, who had bought the Aikens' Drugs from Mrs. Aikens before she died, called Eric into his office in the back of the store. He was a tall, thin man, severe, with little humor, but a decent person who was as cautious with money and the making of prescriptions as he was with people.

"I'm concerned about your mother," he told Eric. "When she first came, she was wonderful and seemed glad to be working after your difficulties. Lately," he said matter-of-factly, "she's had lapses."

"Lapses?"

"I'm not sure what to call them," he said. "From time to time even before your sister ran away, she'd wander around the store as though she were dreaming. I'd say 'Mrs. Walker' and she'd smile at me, nod as though we were just passing on the street or had met each other at a cocktail party."

"You haven't an idea of letting her go," Eric interrupted quickly. "Of course, she's under a strain."

"Of course I won't let her go," Mr. Clark said. "But I wanted you to know because I've been concerned about her."

"I'm sure it will pass," Eric said. "Just as soon as my father's trial is over in June."

He got up to shake Mr. Clark's hand and leave.

"Rebecca pays the rent," Mr. Clark said as Eric was going.

"Mother's capable of it," Eric snapped. "She's just giving Rebecca some responsibility."

"That's all I meant, of course," Mr. Clark said.

*   *   *

"You pay the rent and what else?"

"Everything else. The phone. Liza's lessons. Sarah's. Groceries."

"What about Mother?"

"Eric," Rebecca said, "Mother can't."

"She's a grown woman," Eric said. "She's got a regular size brain, two eyes, two ears, everything to be expected." He got up and went to the window. "She's got to take charge, Rebecca."

"She can't," Rebecca said.

Alicia Walker had been a capable mother, limited by the definition of motherhood, fearful of a world beyond that one of her family which she understood, but capable of providing a home which fulfilled old ideas of home, with large family meals and sunny rooms. It was as though the light from the sun that filled the rooms had been created by the woman who hung the curtains and opened the windows and planted the garden beneath them.

"Mother can't stand the present," Rebecca said. "So she's like an old woman escaping into the past."

"I don't blame her," Eric said. "I would too. You're doing it."

"How am I doing it?"

"By dreaming of heroes."

"Daddy."

"Of course." He sat down, put his feet up, took off his glasses and tossed them on the coffee table beside his legs.

"Don't Eric," Rebecca said. "Leave me alone about him."

"I'll try," Eric said, and for a while he did in spite of a constant inner urging to dismantle Edward Walker especially for Rebecca.

*　*　*

That night, the fifth night Sarah was gone, the fourth night Eric had been home on another leave from medical school, Alicia Walker came out of her bedroom after supper, dressed to go out in the rose taffeta formal and a short black velvet jacket with white rabbit fur around the collar.

"Where, for chrissake, are you going, Mother?" Eric shouted, out of control. "To a masquerade?"

"A masquerade?" Alicia Walker looked confused. "I have a date tonight. He's picking me up at eight."

"A date?" Eric looked at Rebecca. "Do something," he said. "Please."

Rebecca took her mother by the arm and led her back to the lavender-striped bedroom, helping her off with the velvet jacket, the rose taffeta gown, and beneath that a merry widow without stays.

75

"Mother," Rebecca asked, "why do you wear this thing?"

"All the girls wear them," Alicia said, unresistant to Rebecca's help.

* * *

"She has spells," Rebecca said.

" 'Spells' as in 'crazy,' " Eric said, flopping face down on the couch.

"She thinks she's young again," Rebecca said. "Spells like that. Sometimes she thinks she's my age."

"Poor Mother," Eric said, rolling over on his back, putting his legs up on the arms of the couch. "I expect she'd like to be eighteen again and start over. That way she could marry another man, like Tom Bush or John Marshall. Before Dad, she used to go out with Tom Bush."

Eric and Rebecca stayed up until after midnight again Saturday, as they had every night since Sarah had disappeared, hoping for a call from the police or from someone in New York or Connecticut or even from Sarah herself.

"I'm leaving tomorrow," Eric said as Rebecca got up to go to bed.

"Do you have to?"

"I'll flunk out," he said.

"In an emergency, you'll come back?"

"Listen, Rebecca, kids run away for months, for years. I could stay here in this charming little apartment until I grow hair in my ears waiting for Sarah."

Rebecca went into her bedroom, undressed with the light off and climbed in next to Eliza.

"Rebecca?" Eric knocked.

"Yeah."

"In an emergency, I'd come."

"I know," Rebecca said.

She heard him move away from the door.

"Eric," she called. "You could sleep in Sarah's bed," she said. "It's empty."

"Okay," he said, "but I'm getting to love the couch."

8

Sarah had been gone two weeks. Missy Clover said her boyfriend's mother had seen Sarah in Bloomingdale's in New York City. Auntie Ruth had a note from her, which said she was hoping to be accepted at the Ballet Theatre and was living in a hotel. She said to tell Rebecca, which Auntie Ruth did, adding moral messages and dark news of a second cousin twice removed who had been murdered on Eighth Avenue during her lunch hour. Eric contacted the Ballet Theatre, but they had no record of Sarah Walker auditioning. Perhaps she had used a stage name, they said. Eric went himself to New York for a day and watched the company rehearse. Sarah was not in it.

"Just because she wasn't in the company doesn't mean she didn't try out for it," Rebecca said. "There are all kinds of possibilities."

"Yeah," Eric said. "I can think of a hundred terrible ones."

"Not surprising," Rebecca replied.

Edward Walker sat across a wooden table from Rebecca. He sat hunched over, his shoulders raised like a camel's hump, his fingers woven together as tight as tapestry, his eyes shifting from his hands to the window behind Rebecca, never connecting.

"How is Mother?" he asked.

"All right," Rebecca answered, puzzled. "Didn't you see her on Tuesday?"

"No," he said. "She hasn't been here for two weeks."

"But she said she was going," Rebecca said. "She left work early Tuesday, intending to come here."

"Never mind," Edward Walker said with an agitated wave of his hand. "It's just as well if I don't see any of you until the trial."

"Not me?" Rebecca asked.

"Not you."

"But I want to come."

"Come for yourself, then," Edward Walker said.

They didn't discuss Sarah. Rebecca told him the day after Sarah had run away and kept him informed by phone daily on developments, like the note to Auntie Ruth, but on one visit Edward Walker said he didn't want to hear about Sarah at all.

"There's nothing I can do about her in here," he said. "Tell me if she's found or comes home," he said, "or worse."

* * *

"He feels guilty," Eric said. "That's an optimistic sign."

79

"But he's not," Rebecca said.

"I mean guilty about Sarah's leaving home."

"He's not guilty of embezzling," Rebecca said.

"Don't get into this again," Eric said. "You know how I feel."

"But you're wrong," she said, unwilling to give up.

"I could be dead wrong," he said. "I'm thinking of moving to Pakistan next month. They need doctors."

"Oh, shut up, Eric."

* * *

The fact that Michael Ryan was accepted at Yale altered Rebecca's affections for the place.

"You'll never see him," Eric said. "It's a big place."

"Listen, if Mike Ryan and I were at different ends of China together," Rebecca said, "I couldn't miss him."

Michael Ryan was, Rebecca suspected, capable of murder. In fourth grade he had persuaded Denny Jones to jump off the railroad bridge over Main Street. "Or I'll tell everyone you're chicken," he said.

And Denny Jones broke his leg above the hip.

"Mike Ryan dared me," Denny Jones insisted. "He said he'd tell everyone I'm chicken. Besides," he said, "if I hadn't jumped, he would have pushed me."

"He's never blamed," Rebecca told her mother once about Mike Ryan. "He lies like other people tell the truth."

* * *

Lately, since the news from Yale, Mike Ryan made a point of meeting Rebecca after school. When she left by the Roosevelt Street side door in order to miss him, he was standing in front of Aikens' Drugs, waiting for her.

"Do you mind if I come up?" he asked, linking arms with her, confident of advances. He was beautiful to look at, with thick black hair and the clear skin of the northern Irish, tall and slender, with the high buttocks of a natural athlete.

"I don't know why you don't like him," Missy Clover said to Rebecca. "Most girls think he's really incredible."

"Incredibly mean," Rebecca said.

"Yeah," Missy agreed. "But some girls really like that. Besides, he looks wonderful."

"Poor dumb Missy," Sarah had said when Rebecca told her. "She'll end up marrying someone like Michael Ryan."

And after the lights were out that night in the pastel-flowered bedroom, Sarah said, "Y'know, whenever I think of mass murder of the male population, I have a clear picture of Michael Ryan."

* * *

"I have to take Eliza to piano," Rebecca said, retrieving her arm from Michael Ryan's.

"I just saw Eliza leave," Mike said, "with Mrs. Cupp."

"Well," Rebecca hedged.

"Just for a while," Mike said. "To talk about Yale and stuff."

Rebecca made iced tea and they sat in the window seat overlooking Main Street.

"Any word from Sarah?"

"Nope," Rebecca said.

"Sarah's a funny girl," Mike said. "I've never known anyone our age so caught up in a career. That's what you think she's doing now, isn't it? I heard she was trying for a dancing job in New York."

"We think so," Rebecca said. "She's very good," she added defensively, as though Mike Ryan had challenged her.

"I know she's good," he said. "I mean 'funny' because she hates men."

The statement was matter-of-fact, but the nature of it intruded on Rebecca's sensibilities. It was as though Michael Ryan knew their private lives, as if he understood what she was just beginning to understand: that Sarah Walker's dislike of men was bound to her dark feeling about Edward Walker, just as Rebecca's susceptibility was bound to her love for her father.

Rebecca followed Michael Ryan when he got up to look through Eric's record collection, which he had kept even though the stereo was sold at auction. She stood next to him, reading the jacket titles over his shoulder. Something in the way that Mike Ryan stood angered Rebecca, one foot resting on the chair, thumbing through the albums, as though he was conscious of the way he looked to her. There he stood, intruding on Eric's things, searching for family secrets perhaps, probably disdainful of them all, thinking in his beautiful head that he graced the blighted Walkers with his presence.

"It's too bad," he said sympathetically, looking her in the eye with another message, which wasn't necessarily sympathetic, "what's happened to you guys."

And Rebecca turned on him, uncaged, ignited by her dark dreams.

"He's not guilty," she shouted, jumping on Michael Ryan's back, pulling his black curly hair, and then, out of control, she bit the back of his neck, gripping the warm flesh like dough between her teeth.

"For chrissake!" he shouted. "Jesus Christ!" he cried, but she didn't let go until he'd hit her so hard on the back that she had to let go in order to cry out.

He put his hand behind his neck, wiped the wound with his palm and looked at it.

"Blood," he said. "It's a regular animal farm here," he yelled, and ran down the steps, out the front door and up Main Street.

* * *

"I bit Mike Ryan," Rebecca said when Eric called to tell her about Sarah.

"You honestly bit him?"

"In the back of the neck until it bled."

"Rebecca," he said quietly.

"I thought you'd laugh."

"Laugh?"

"You laughed when I told you I'd thought about it," she said, crying. "You thought it was very funny then."

"Listen, Rebecca, you're the most calm and

83

sensible woman I know. If we were attacked by the British who'd lost their sense of time, you're the only woman I'd count on to lead us to victory."

"Don't tease, Eric. Please don't tease. I feel awful."

"Rebecca," Eric said quietly. "Our family's reputation is in question. If people are in danger of being bitten when they come to visit—"

"We haven't heard from Sarah," Rebecca interrupted.

"That's why I called," Eric said. "I have."

Sarah had gone to New York by bus from New Canaan and spent that night in Grand Central Station. The next morning she went to the Ballet Theatre and asked about auditions. She said her name was Alicia DuPres and that she was eighteen. The first afternoon she had met a teacher and choreographer, who took her home to her apartment at West Fifty-fourth. That's where she had been since. She had danced two nights in the chorus of *Coppelia*, and otherwise she had gone daily, hoping for another chance to replace a dancer who was ill. But now she was coming home, Eric said, and would be on the eight o'clock train.

"Meet her," Eric said. "I can tell something happened in New York."

"How come she called you?"

"Because, Rebec, she's afraid of you," Eric said patiently. "You're the model child. She hasn't learned about your career in biting."

* * *

Sarah was thinner than when she had left, with black circles under her eyes and too much makeup. She was wearing the same clothes she had left for the gymnastics tournament in, and carried a dancing bag.

"Don't say anything," Sarah said when she got off the train.

They walked up Main Street together without speaking. Occasionally Rebecca glanced at her younger sister, surprised at how old she'd become in two weeks, at the odd fix of her jaw, her hair pulled back so tight it altered the flesh on her face.

"Is Mother at home?" Sarah asked when they got to Aikens' Drugs.

"Yes," Rebecca said. "And Eliza."

"Is she the same?"

"Pretty much," Rebecca said.

They stood together under the artificial lights of Aikens' Drugs, the round red lights advertising WHITMAN'S CHOCOLATES, the neon lights protecting the prescription counter after the store was closed.

"I don't want to discuss my leaving," Sarah said. "Promise me it'll be as if I never left."

"I promise," she said and followed Sarah up the steps to the apartment.

9

Edward Walker's trial was set for the beginning of June, and there was plenty of talk about it in Old Greenwich.

"People are delighted with the misfortunes of others," Edward Walker told Rebecca one afternoon when she met him after school.

"Don't expect sympathy for us," he told her another day. "The majority of my friends are hoping I'll get fifteen years."

"You're bitter," Rebecca said.

"Honest, Rebecca," he said. "Not bitter."

But Rebecca noticed her father was withdrawn, that many days there were long spaces between conversations. He seemed to have lost interest in the lives of his children. She assumed it was the trial and believed that when the trial was over with its inevitable positive outcome, he would be himself again.

"Steel yourself for the worst," he'd tell her.

She tried. She'd act out the worst prospect in her mind, pretend that he was found guilty and sentenced to a minimum of five years, but the imaginings were not believable, like ghost stories became when she was old enough to disbelieve in ghosts. Mostly she steeled herself for the end of May and the trial itself. She didn't believe in miracles. She simply expected that her father would come home and work again, that her mother would get better, that they'd live modestly in a simple house, perhaps on Roosevelt or Lincoln Avenue, that in the fall she would go to Yale. Her expectations, it seemed to her, were not excessive. Except for biting Michael Ryan, she had been exceptional and deserved reasonable expectations. Or so she told herself.

In May she learned that Yale had offered her full scholarship plus a stipend.

"I hear Yale's paying you to go there," Mike Ryan said to her one afternoon. "I wonder if they know you bite."

It had been all over school. Mike Ryan had a bandage the size of a football on the back of his neck and growled at Rebecca when they passed in the hall. On her locker, someone had put a sign: MUZZLE YOUR DOG. OLD GREENWICH POLICE DEPARTMENT. She left it there.

Missy Clover stopped her after trigonometry and asked if it was true.

"Of course it's true," Rebecca answered.

"I did," Rebecca said to the counselor at the high school, "and I might do it again."

* * *

"You really bit him?" Sarah had asked one night.

"Yes," she'd said.

"Rebecca."

"Well," Rebecca said, "you can't blame me."

Sarah sat on the bed across from her sister and watched her in disbelief.

"It's just not like you," she said. "Do you think you're falling apart?"

It had occurred to Rebecca. For several nights after it had happened, she reenacted the scene in her head before she went to sleep at night, hoping to discover the moment she lost control, as if by finding that moment she could prevent its reoccurrence. But always she saw Mike Ryan thumbing through Eric's albums and the next immediate scene was the thick flesh on the back of Michael Ryan's neck with her teeth marks in half-moons around it.

She decided mechanically that if she was in danger of falling apart, she'd have to use specific measures to take control. She ordered her day with long lists. She spent an hour with Eliza, helping her with homework, she listened to the radio with Sarah although they seldom spoke, she wrote Eric daily, she did extra homework and relieved her mother for two hours twice a week.

"I'll take your job in the summer," she suggested to Alicia Walker. "I spoke with Mr. Clark about it and he agreed."

It had, in fact, been Mr. Clark's idea. He'd called Rebecca to his office one afternoon while she was working and suggested that Alicia needed the summer to repair. "She can go to the beach," he suggested.

"Lie in the sun. She can use my Sunfish if you've had to sell your boat."

Surprisingly, Alicia resisted.

"I wouldn't know what to do with myself all day," she said.

"You need rest," Rebecca said.

"But"—Alicia laughed, an odd, indifferent laugh—"from what excitement? You get another job and then we can send Eliza to camp. Maybe Sarah can get a job, since she's given up dancing."

Sarah had to stop dancing for a week after she returned from New York City because she strained a ligament in her calf. All afternoon and evening after school, she'd lie face down on her bed in the pastel-flowered bedroom with a heating pad on the back of her leg. She didn't even read. By the second week she'd taken off the heating pad, but still she spent the evenings face down on her bed. Occasionally she slept.

The ballet teacher, whose name was Monique, called every day. Sarah wouldn't go to the phone.

"Still not better?" Monique asked.

"No."

"At least have her come and watch," she said. "She can learn something."

But Sarah simply shrugged and wouldn't practice.

One night Rebecca couldn't stand the change in Sarah any longer, and while Eliza was out of the room she begged Sarah to tell her what happened in New York.

"You promised not to ask," Sarah said archly and

left the room. "Maybe you think I'm being peculiar, but I just prefer it this way."

* * *

Eric was in earnest sick. "Pneumonia," he said triumphantly from the hospital.

"Is it serious?"

"Of course it's serious," Eric said, annoyed. "I had a temperature of a hundred and six."

"A hundred and three," Gayatri said when Rebecca called her. "But he is sick," she insisted. "He should wear overshoes in the rain."

"I caught it from a patient, not rain," he said.

"There could be complications," he said another time when Rebecca called.

"Gayatri says you got your feet wet."

"Christ," Eric said. "That's the trouble with places like Pakistan where you go straight to medical school without college," he said. "No common sense."

He got out of the hospital at the beginning of June.

"The doctor suggested I come home to rest," he said on the telephone. "I didn't embarrass the family by describing the kind of rest I'd get in the apartment over Aikens' Drugs."

"You'll be home in time for Dad?" Rebecca asked.

"For the trial," he said. "Of course."

They planned to take turns going to the trial, since it could go on for days. Only Eliza wouldn't be allowed to go.

"I *know* everything," Eliza said.

"I'll take you once when Mother's working," Rebecca said, "if you won't tell."

"It's Mother who shouldn't go," Eliza said.

And she was right.

* * *

On the Sunday morning two weeks before Edward Walker's trial was scheduled to begin, Rebecca got a call from the police station at Old Greenwich. They said they had found Alicia Walker on Main Street at four in the morning, and would Rebecca come to the station to collect her.

Rebecca went alone. Alicia Walker sat in a side room on a wooden bench with her hands folded in her lap. She had on the rose taffeta formal and silver shoes, her hair was tied back in a ribbon, and she was holding a dogwood branch.

"Tore that from the bushes on Lincoln Avenue," the officer said. "And she won't give it up."

10

Mrs. Robert Hanson, whose husband ran Christ Church on Main Street, organized a committee to support the Walker children. She worked with great speed and came to see Rebecca about arrangements only two days after Alicia Walker had been hospitalized in the state hospital in New Haven.

"The Lueders have offered to take Eliza," Mrs. Hanson said. "It will be much better for her to be in a family situation."

"She's in a family situation," Rebecca said. "Her own."

"Oh, dearie," Mrs. Hanson said, "you know what I mean. Regular meals, adult supervision."

"We're fine," Rebecca insisted.

"Now, Rebecca." Mrs. Hanson put her hand on Rebecca's arm. "Don't be falsely proud. You're not fine," she said.

Later Rebecca guessed that Mrs. Hanson had heard about her biting Michael Ryan. It could, she suspected, have been a subject in Sunday school class.

"I thought the dance teacher could take Sarah," Mrs. Hanson said.

"Sarah isn't dancing," Rebecca said matter-of-factly.

"We've gotten together," Mrs. Hanson said.

"We're staying here," Rebecca said. "The three of us, and Eric will be back in a week."

"We've formed a committee," Mrs. Hanson insisted, but Rebecca walked her to the front door.

"I expected you to be more grown up," Mrs. Hanson said. "To accept your limitations."

That night, at Rebecca's request, Eric called Mrs. Hanson from Cambridge and suggested that her committee research another cause.

The following afternoon Mrs. Hanson reported to her members that she'd been unsuccessful in her approach to the Walker children, that certainly the children would not survive without assistance, and that they would have to find another solution.

*　*　*

Rebecca bought her father a pin-striped shirt for Father's Day, which he opened quickly and set aside without examining.

"We have never celebrated Father's day before," he said, but stopped when he saw the expression on Rebecca's face.

"You know about Mother," Rebecca said.

"Bob Hanson called," he said. "I had her moved today."

"Moved where?"

"To a private place called Manor Lodge, outside of Middletown."

"We can't afford it," Rebecca said quickly.

"Have you ever seen a state mental hospital?" Edward Walker asked. "Of course we can afford it."

"How?" Rebecca asked, surprised at her boldness in questioning her father as she had never done.

"I've managed things for years, Rebecca," Edward Walker said. "It's no different now, whatever the circumstances."

She didn't pursue the conversation. She had been managing things too—paying the bills, caring for Eliza and Sarah, providing. Rebecca knew how much money there was, and it wasn't much. Enough to live daily from Alicia Walker's inheritance, a survival portion set aside from the sale of the house, but not a lot. Not enough for the private hospitalization of her mother. Or for Yale.

Driving home that afternoon from prison, Rebecca was conscious for the first time of an insisting doubt of her father. She hadn't thought that he was capable of deception, and he was. She knew he was. But she threw it out of her head like an irritating pebble before it could settle and disturb her sleep.

*   *   *

Mrs. Robert Hanson called that evening to invite the Walker girls to a benefit dance at the country club as her guests. She insisted. Rebecca couldn't think of a legitimate excuse.

"To a benefit dance at the country club," Sarah said. "Not me."

"We have to," Rebecca said. "To save face."

"A wonderful reason," Sarah said. "As if we had any worth saving."

"To benefit what?" Eric asked on the telephone that night.

"I don't know," Sarah said.

"Ask."

"I did," she said. "Mrs. Hanson said it was for a hospital."

"No," Eric said. "The answer is no. I try to limit my trips from medical school to matters of importance, like runaways and nervous breakdowns. Not benefit dances."

"Well," Rebecca said, "I'm going."

"Have a terrific time," Sarah said.

*　*　*

Missy Clover told Rebecca about Sarah one afternoon at Aikens' Drugs, where Rebecca had taken her mother's place at the cash register. She was given permission by the principal to miss the last two weeks of school, and Mr. Clark promised her time off for graduation and the trial.

Missy Clover was at the makeup counter trying on blush when she saw Rebecca and told her that Sarah hadn't been in school for a week.

"Hasn't anyone told you?" Missy asked, deciding on "Splendid Peach."

"Nope," Rebecca said. "Sarah leaves before I do. She walks Eliza to grammar school and then goes on to the high school."

"Well, she never gets there," Missy said.

* * *

Sarah was always at home and in her room when Rebecca came home from work. She hadn't returned to gymnastics or even to dancing, but occasionally she practiced in the living room.

The morning after Missy Clover told her, Rebecca was waiting in the house at quarter past nine when Sarah got back from taking Eliza to school.

"What are you doing back?" Rebecca asked.

"I could ask you the same question."

"I waited because Missy said you hadn't been in school for a week."

"A week and a half," Sarah said, dropping her books on the kitchen chair. "Missy's losing her touch."

"Everyone is watching us," Rebecca said. "They're expecting us not to make it."

"Well," Sarah said, taking a banana from the top of the refrigerator, "we're obliging them."

* * *

Mrs. Robert Hanson was not "simple-minded," as Sarah insisted, but her understanding of people was limited to a conventional view of them, uncomplicated. She was condemning when people behaved, as they often did, unpredictably, out of fear perhaps. It was not vindictive. She was, however, a woman of enormous energy and power in a small town. People were careful to appear quite ordinary around her, considerate of the fact that she had a strong sense of her own rightness and an intolerance of eccentricities.

When she called Rebecca, suggesting that she and

Sarah bring escorts, Rebecca was afraid to tell her that Sarah had no intention of coming.

"You have to," Rebecca said. "I can't explain why. Mother would expect us to," she added carefully, knowing that Sarah might respond to that. "You don't have to bring an escort," Rebecca said. "I'm not. Or you could try to convince Eric to come."

"Incest," Sarah said. "Something the Walkers haven't thought of."

* * *

Rebecca and Sarah went to the dance in dresses borrowed from Missy Clover's cousin Madge, made up with painted smiles, eyes shadowed and circled in black, barely recognizable as their former selves.

"I'd prefer to wear a panther costume," Sarah said.

"Do you think I look like a prostitute?" Rebecca asked, inspecting herself before they left for the dance.

"Not enough," Sarah said. "You can do better."

They got to the country club late after cocktails, and they could see as they walked down the hall to the main dining room that already people were seated at tables for dinner. Even before they reached the door, Mrs. Robert Hanson spotted them and hurried through the room to greet them, followed by Patty Miller at her heels.

"Welcome," she said, kissing them both. "It's wonderful to see you."

Miss Henderson from the library was there and Annie Street, Alicia's childhood friend, and Tuffy

Slaughter, who was Alicia's cousin, all greeting Sarah and Rebecca Walker with unaccountable enthusiasm in the corridor of the country club as though they expected something of them.

"We're so proud of you," Patty said, patting Sarah's back. "You're doing wonderfully."

"We were just talking at my table," Miss Henderson the librarian was saying, "about the remarkable courage of children. A book should be written."

"Does she mean for us to write it?" Sarah whispered later to Rebecca after they were seated at a table with friends from town their own age.

Johnny Barber was there with a girl from boarding school who no one knew, and he danced with Rebecca before she sat down for dinner. Like Rebecca, he had a respectable reputation as a fine young man, responsible, productive, not extraordinary but absolutely reliable. They had been friends since childhood, had flirted in the last two years with a kind of romance, but they were both shy by nature and cautious, so nothing had developed. Since the situation with Edward Walker, Rebecca wanted Johnny's high opinion of her, as though his opinion was representative of the town's. Now, as he danced with her, she sensed something unfamiliar in him. She sensed a judgment in his touch.

"What's the matter with you?" she asked as they sat down.

He shrugged.

"You're strange tonight. Like a mannequin."

"It's the dance, I guess," he said. "The whole idea gives me the creeps."

"What's the whole idea?" Rebecca asked, on guard. "It's the usual boring country club dance, isn't it?"

He looked at her in surprise.

"Rebecca," he said, and then quickly, consciously, he added, "of course. I hate these things, that's all, and my parents make me come."

But Rebecca knew that she had caught Johnny Barber unaware and that this wasn't an ordinary country club dance.

"What's going on?" Rebecca asked Sarah in the ladies' room.

"I don't know," Sarah said. "But somehow this whole evening has to do with us. I can feel it."

"How?"

"People are looking at us."

"Staring?"

"Just looking. That's bad enough."

"Ask Missy Clover," Rebecca said.

* * *

Missy Clover could be counted on to deliver any bad news. And she was glad this evening to provide Sarah Walker with all the details she knew about the benefit dance.

Rebecca went with Sarah down the back steps of the club, which led to the pool.

"It's for Mother," Sarah said even before they were out of earshot of the guests standing on the porch.

"I don't understand."

"The goddamned dance," Sarah said. "It's for

Mother. To raise the money to pay for her at Manor Lodge, and every single person here knows it but us."

Rebecca sat down on the bottom step.

"Were they going to tell us?"

"They expected that we'd find out," Sarah said. "But they were afraid we wouldn't come if we knew. A surprise party."

"What are you going to do?"

"I'm going home."

"No."

"Do you think I'd go back in there?"

"No," Rebecca said.

"Talk to me," Sarah said, and took her hand. "Please say something."

But Rebecca couldn't talk. Instinctively she wanted to do something terrible, to walk in the ballroom absolutely naked or set fire to Mrs. Robert Hanson's closet, to tell her father. He'd do something, she thought quickly. He'd know just what to do.

"I'm not going back," Sarah said again.

"You don't have to," Rebecca said.

"Are you?"

Rebecca stood up and walked back up the stairs.

"Rebec?"

"I'll meet you in a while in the ladies' room," she said. "You can hide in there if you want to."

"You're going to say you know what's up?"

"Nope," Rebecca said. "I'm not going to say a thing. And tomorrow, I'm going to tell Daddy."

Sarah followed her up the stairs.

"He knows," she said. "Missy said he'd agreed to this thing."

"I don't believe you," Rebecca said. "He wouldn't. He's too proud."

"There's a limit to how proud you can be from prison," Sarah said.

* * *

Rebecca met Sarah at midnight. She was sitting in one of the stalls of the bathroom with her feet up.

"Reverend Hanson has offered to drive us home," she said to Sarah. "He's concerned about street dangers."

"Let's walk," Sarah said, "and pray for street dangers." Walking down Main Street, she took her sister's hand in an unexpected gesture they had left behind in childhood.

11

The week before the trial, the newspapers were full of stories. There was a story about the benefit ball, with a picture of Mrs. Robert Hanson holding a check for three thousand dollars.

"You girls have so much on your mind," Mrs. Hanson had said to Rebecca several days after the dance. "I'll handle the hospital expenses."

"She thought you'd steal it," Eric said.

"I would have," Sarah said.

The article mentioned all of the children by name and said that the benefit was to pay for special hospitalization for Alicia Walker. It did not mention the nature of her illness.

"Leprosy," Sarah said.

"Mother doesn't have leprosy," Eliza said. "Americans don't get leprosy."

"We all have it," Sarah said, grabbing Eliza's arm, pointing to a scab on her elbow. "See. We are the first native-born Americans to have leprosy on our natural soil."

"I got that falling off Dickie Marriott's bike," Eliza said.

"Jesus, Sarah," Eric said. "It's a regular funeral when you're around."

"Not me," Sarah said. "I have the only positive attitude in the family." She sat down next to Eric. "I think we should order up a tank of oxygen from Aikens'," she said. "You look like you need it."

"How come?"

"You're getting a little blue."

Eric got up and looked in the bathroom mirror. He turned on the light and looked again.

"What do you think?" Sarah asked when he came back in the room.

"I think you're color blind," he said.

*   *   *

There was an article with pictures of Edward Walker's career. It showed a high school picture from his yearbook, a college picture of his cross country team, his graduation picture and several pictures of him since he had married and moved to Old Greenwich, one with Rebecca on a bicycle.

"Did you see the family album?" Eric asked Sarah. "We ought to keep clippings for future generations of our kind."

"You know," Eliza said, sitting on the couch next to Eric, "I hate it when Rebecca's working."

"And when I'm home?" Sarah asked.

"No," Eliza said. "Not exactly."

"What about when I'm home?" Eric asked.

"You get sick too much," Eliza said. "You used to

be funny and a little sick, and now you're all the time sick and not so funny."

"What you mean to say is that Rebecca is nicer to you than we are," Eric said, sitting up, tucking in his shirttails.

"I mean to say," Eliza said, weeping now, "I like it better when Rebecca isn't working."

"Eliza is miserable," Rebecca said that night at supper.

"In this lighthearted family," Eric said, "I can't imagine it."

Rebecca hit his fingers with a spoon.

"Watch out," Sarah said. "Rebecca Walker bites." She ate half her yogurt and put it back in the refrigerator. "I can't eat. Everything tastes like milk of magnesia."

"We'll be terrific at the trial," Rebecca said. "Liza will cry. Eric will be carried out on a stretcher with cardiac arrest."

"Eliza's going?" Eric asked.

"She wants to," Rebecca said.

"So she can store up on childhood memories."

"That's what I mean by sticking together," Rebecca said. "For Liza's sake."

"Rebecca's right," Eric said, slamming his hand on the table. "United we stand," he growled. "Divided we fall." He took a broom and marched around the room with it. *"United we stand."* He put it to melody. *"Di-vided* we fall," he sang. *"U-n-i-ted* we stand." He clicked his heels together. Sarah got up to leave the kitchen, but he grabbed her by the shoulders and barked, *"Divided we fall."*

Rebecca left the kitchen, walked through the living room and down the stairs onto Main Street.

Eliza was spending the night at the Leuders', and Aikens' Drugs was closed. Mike Ryan sat in his car in front of the liquor store with two other boys.

"What are you doing?" he called to Rebecca.

"Nothing," she answered.

"Want to come to Hal Scott's?" he asked. "There's a party."

She hesitated.

"Come on." He grabbed her hand playfully.

"I guess not," she said. "I'm in a bad mood."

"It's a bad week coming up," he said.

She didn't reply. The library was still open and she went in.

"Do you need books for your father this week?" Miss Hildenbrand asked from below the main desk, where she was sorting books.

"No thanks," Rebecca said.

"I guess this will be a busy week for him," she said.

The mother of the Farmer family who had bought the Walkers' house on the Sound was there, and she stopped Rebecca.

"We love the house," she said.

"We did too," Rebecca said.

"How do you like being in the center of town in your new place?"

"It's awful," Rebecca said coolly.

"I'm sorry." The woman reached out to touch her. "That was thoughtless of me."

But Rebecca was out the front door of the library and down the steps by the time the woman left. She ducked behind the Graysons' magnolia tree, which was low to the ground and in bloom.

"Rebecca?" She heard the woman call, but she didn't answer.

For a while, she sat under the tree in the Graysons' side yard until the traffic thinned on Main Street, the sounds of voices on the porches were gone, Miss Hildenbrand had locked up the library for the night, and the Graysons had turned off the lights on the first floor and gone upstairs. It must have been after ten, which meant she'd have to walk an empty Main Street back to the apartment.

She may be counting on too much for Edward Walker's trial, she decided. She wanted a declaration of innocence, proclaimed with white flags and marching in the streets, with banner headlines in *The New York Times* so every person who had suspected the worst of her father would know. For that, she was glad to stay in the apartment above Aikens' Drugs, to delay college or even not to go to Yale at all, to work at the prescription counter until her father built his business again. Every conscious part of Rebecca Walker seemed inextricably bound to a declaration of Edward Walker's innocence as if without it, without a public statement, she was insubstantial as dandelion silk.

*   *   *

"You can't hang everything on that, Rebecca," Eric said that night when she came home. "What if the jury finds, for whatever reason, that he must have embezzled. You'll go to pieces."

She sat across from him on the couch in the dark.

"Maybe," she said.

"You have to believe what you believe," he said. "You can't expect to be vindicated."

"You don't believe he's innocent."

Eric sat on the couch with his feet on the table.

"Well?" she insisted.

"You know I don't."

"Nor does Sarah."

"Ask her."

The door to Sarah's room was shut and the light was off. Faintly Rebecca could hear music from the radio.

"I don't need to," Rebecca said.

* * *

There was a letter for Sarah Monday morning from the Ballet Theatre addressed to Alicia DuPres. It was full of praise for her talent and offered her a place in the school for the following fall.

Sarah was in bed under the covers with a pillow over her head.

"Sarah," Rebecca called. "That's wonderful about your letter."

"Shut up," Sarah said from under the pillow.

* * *

The doctors at Manor Lodge told the children that Alicia Walker could not have visitors until mid-July.

"Absolutely no strife," they said, "and we're confident she'll be out by the end of the summer."

"She's knitting baby clothes," Eric told Rebecca. "That puts her at about twenty-two, so she's aged four years since she went in. By August, she could be forty-five again."

* * *

Eric went to see Edward Walker the night before the trial. He went alone. His father had requested it.

"What happened?" Rebecca asked when he came home.

Eric was evasive.

"Steel yourself for the worst," he said.

"Those are exactly Daddy's words to me," she said.

"He's not optimistic, Rebec."

"Are you?"

"Am I ever optimistic?"

"What a gloomy family," Rebecca said. "We'd have been perfect early Christians. Death, deprivation, despair. Can you imagine how blissful you would have found it in the first century?"

"I'm being honest," Eric said, "not negative."

"I believe there's a chance."

"Okay, okay, believe in anything you like. Life after death, the transmigration of souls, the immaculate conception."

"Go to bed, Eric," Rebecca said. "You'll get high blood pressure."

"Too late, sweetheart," he said to her with a fake punch. "I have it already."

Rebecca opened the door to her bedroom.

"Check the dancer's corpse for vital signs," Eric said, and then he checked her himself. Rebecca watched him lean over Sarah, whose eyes were closed although she wasn't sleeping, brush her hair out of her eyes, and pull a cover around her shoulders. "Poor chicks," he whispered almost inaudibly.

12

Unexpectedly, the trial of Edward Walker for the embezzlement of private funds lasted only two days. On the first day, Rebecca went with Eric to Bridgeport, which was the county seat.

"I couldn't sleep last night," Rebecca said at breakfast. "I can't eat, either."

"As usual, I feel wonderful," Eric said stretching until his chalk-white belly showed beneath his shirt.

"Yik," Eliza said. "Your stomach looks like dough."

"It's a perfectly fine stomach in tip-top shape," Eric said. "A little pale, perhaps."

"You're late for school," Rebecca said, hurrying Eliza.

"What about Sarah?" Liza asked. "Isn't she going to school?"

"I thought Sarah was going with us," Eric said.

"Are you kidding?" Rebecca cleared the table. "Sarah hasn't seen Daddy once since April. She wouldn't consider coming."

When Rebecca went in the bedroom they shared, Sarah was sleeping.

"Are you going to school?" Rebecca asked.

Sarah shook her head.

"How come?"

"I'm sick," Sarah said.

"You're chicken."

"Then I'm chicken."

"You can't hide from everything."

"Don't," Sarah began.

"It gives me the creeps to see you sleeping all the time."

Sarah sat up, pulled the covers over her shoulders. "I am sick," she said. "Pressed, I may throw up."

"Don't press," Eric called from the living room. "I have limits."

* * *

Rebecca walked Eliza to school.

"What's going to happen today?" Eliza asked.

"They'll present the case on both sides. Daddy's and the state's."

"Will Daddy speak?"

"Not today," Rebecca said. "Maybe tomorrow. Surely Wednesday, when we're taking you."

"Are you scared?"

"I feel queer," Rebecca said. "Sarah and Eric are driving me crazy." She took Eliza's hand and they walked down Main together. The sun was hot, the day already more uncomfortable than usual in June. The streets were full of cars headed towards the turnpike, tooting goodbyes, and children, especially high school students, lingered on street corners as though if they waited long enough, the term would be over before they reached the high school.

"You'll go back home with Janie Leuders," Rebecca said. The Leuders had been solid in their support of the Walker children and unobtrusive. "They'll give you dinner."

"Can I spend the night?"

"Nope. I'll pick you up. You know, we have to stick together."

"United we stand." Eliza imitated Eric from days before, and then she saw Janie Leuders and ran ahead, waving goodbye to Rebecca.

"See you tonight," she called back lightly as though with Janie Leuders at her side she could easily dismiss the black promises of the first day of her father's trial.

* * *

"Sarah did throw up," Eric said triumphantly, as if he had caused it.

"Splendid," Rebecca replied.

Sarah was lying on her side with all of the covers pulled up under her chin.

"I'm shivering," she said.

"It's boiling," Rebecca replied. "Do you think you have stomach flu?" she asked, sitting down beside her sister.

"I don't know," Sarah said.

"Do you want me to call someone to stay with you?"

"I'm not going to die."

"That's a possibility we must all consider," Eric said, but he brought her tea and propped her up with pillows and called Patty Miller to check in on her a couple of times while he was gone.

*   *   *

Edward Walker came in with his attorney, wearing the pin-striped shirt Rebecca had given him the last time she'd seen him. He was impeccable. To look at him, it didn't seem possible that he was capable of jaywalking. He sat immobile, leaning over occasionally to listen to his attorney, nodding or shaking his head in response. He never spoke. From time to time, Rebecca tried to catch his eyes, but he didn't seem to be aware that she was there. Or if he was, he didn't acknowledge her.

*   *   *

"It wasn't bad," Rebecca said to Eric when they got home.

"What did you expect?" he asked, unlocking the front door.

"I expected it to be awful," she said. "Somehow, I didn't expect to make it through the morning." She threw her purse on the table, put down a bag of groceries.

"I'm glad for you," Eric said. "I have had better days."

He checked in the bedroom and Sarah wasn't there.

"Sarah," he called. He knocked on the door to his mother's room, which had not been used since she was hospitalized. "She's bolted," he said. But when he opened the door of the lavender-striped bedroom, Sarah was sitting on her mother's bed in her mother's robe, in the hushed gray light of late afternoon.

"Monique came all the way from New York," she said.

"What for?" Rebecca asked.

"To force me to go back," she said. "She said I was letting her down and ruining my chances."

"I'll call her," Eric said. "But I wish you'd tell us what happened in New York."

"She acts as though I'm her possession," Sarah said. "Nothing happened in New York! Don't you understand? You seem to think there was some obvious catastrophe. It wasn't that simple. Monique tried to take over my life, as if she were in the business of purchasing dancers."

"Or daughters," Eric said.

"You should have bitten her," Eric said, but Sarah didn't laugh. When Eric left to call the dance teacher, she fell in Rebecca's lap, and Rebecca held her in her arms as though she were a child until she fell asleep.

* * *

After supper, Eric stood before the window of Rebecca's room, facing Main Street. The lights were off and he was smoking. Eliza was asleep in the bed with Rebecca, and Sarah was in her mother's bed, where she had fallen asleep before dinner.

"You've been keeping me awake," Rebecca said.

"You sleep like a lamb these days?"

"There isn't a chance to sleep like anything with

114

you pacing the floor. What's the matter?"

"Nothing," he said. In the gray light of dusk, he looked like a lacrosse stick in pajamas, nearly comic, thin, without interruptions of flesh. His glasses dominated his face, reflected on his skin. It was, she knew, a look he wanted to invest his temperament with as well, the look of a mildly comic clown, and so his arch remarks, even his make-believe illnesses, were protections of a nature raw-nerved by the impositions of the world.

"I mean, what *new* is the matter," she said, but she said it gently.

Eric sat down at the end of her bed.

"I have this feeling that the trial will be over tomorrow," he said.

"Based on what?" she asked, sitting up.

"Based on a feeling," he said. "That's all."

"People in the final stages of terminal illnesses can't be counted on to know their feelings."

"You're still convinced he's innocent," Eric said, disregarding her.

"If I weren't," she said, "I'd die."

"Oh, shit."

"Go to bed, Eric," she said, "and shut off your gloomy predictions until this whole thing is over."

* * *

When Rebecca got up the next morning, Sarah was dressed.

"I'm going," she said when Rebecca came in the kitchen.

115

"To the trial?"

"It's got to be better than a visit from my dance teacher."

"You could go to school."

"While my father's on trial for embezzling from the parents of half my class?" She took an apple from a bowl on the window sill.

"Falsely accused," Rebecca snapped.

"Maybe," Sarah said, buttoning the back of Eliza's dress.

* * *

Edward Walker took the stand shortly after the morning session began. Immediately Rebecca sensed that things would not go well. He was dressed as he had been dressed the day before, his hair in place, his face pale and clean-shaven as it had not always been when she'd visited him in jail. He looked exactly as he had looked every morning that she could remember before he left for work, wonderful and strong. She was touched to see him standing in front of the courtroom, his side to her, his chin slightly forward, defiant, as she had seen it many times. His voice when he spoke was clear but not altogether steady.

Rebecca was conscious of folding her hands together in her lap. She was conscious of breathing as though she might, without warning, stop. On one side of her, Eric pressed his shoulder against her side. On the other, she could hear Sarah breathing deeply through her nose.

She listened to the judge. She heard him list the charges and ask for her father's plea to them, but it was as though his voice were a distant church bell drowned out occasionally by the traffic in her own mind.

She was watching her father's attorney lean forward on the bench where he was sitting, put his chin in his hands, shake invisible hair off his forehead, when her father answered to the charges. At first, she didn't hear his answer, heard instead the response in the courtroom to his answer, the quiet alteration in the crowd, as though they were whistling in surprise.

"Guilty," he said. "I plead guilty to the charges against me," he said in a voice reverberating like the thin string wires of thought in Rebecca Walker's brain.

13

"Well," Eric said, linking arms with Sarah, "we made it."

"Barely," Sarah replied. "Did you know?"

"He was better off pleading guilty to the charges," Eric said quietly. "Especially since he was."

"You mean they'll be more lenient with him."

"Probably," Eric said. "He looks well, don't you think?"

"Thin," Sarah said, "and distracted."

They ordered cokes. Other people who had been in the courtroom stopped by the delicatessen as well and nodded towards Eric and Sarah in the back booth.

"Celebrities," Eric said, resting his head in folded arms. "I'm not interested in fame. I prefer money and motherly attention."

"I can feel Mrs. Bralove staring at the back of my head," Sarah said.

"Checking for lice," Eric said.

They were waiting at the restaurant for Rebecca, but they didn't talk about her, talked lightly instead of incidentals, as though it were an ordinary morning in their lives and Rebecca was of no more than ordinary concern.

* * *

The trial for Edward Walker ended shortly after he entered his plea of guilty. He was sentenced to five years imprisonment and required, as had been expected, to repay his debts. But Rebecca had left before the judge's decision, had left, in fact, just after her father's plea of guilty. Sarah had found her in the ladies' room.

She was sitting on a plastic couch and looked like pictures from a convent school graduation, the way her hands were folded, her legs crossed at the ankles. She was uncommonly pale.

"You okay?" Sarah asked.

"Perfectly," Rebecca replied.

"Listen, Rebec," she said, "you've got to be okay."

"I said I'm perfectly okay."

"We have to count on you," Sarah said, noticing that Rebecca's eyes were set like her mother's had been from time to time before the illness. "Eliza is counting on you," she said, desperate, willing to use tricks.

"Just leave me alone," Rebecca said.

"If you promise me."

"I promise you I'm perfectly okay."

"You're not going to be sick, are you?" Sarah asked.

"I've never felt better in my life," Rebecca said coldly, looking at her sister for the first time. "I'm in

119

the full bloom of health," she said. "I must be pregnant," she said with an edge of hysteria. "I hear you feel wonderful when you're pregnant."

"Pregnant?" Sarah asked confused.

"Listen, Sarah. Go away."

"Have you done anything to get pregnant?" Sarah insisted.

"Behind the prescription counter at Aikens'? In our living room? For chrissake, when have I had time? I'm kidding you. Ha ha ha ha. That kind of kidding. I'm trying hard not to disintegrate in the ladies' room of the courtroom. Now, will you please go away?"

"Okay," Sarah said. "If you promise." But she left quickly without waiting for an answer.

* * *

"So," Eric said.

"If something has happened to Rebecca—"

"It's her own fault," Eric said.

"Not really."

Eric took his glasses off, cleaned them with a napkin. "She had to believe in him," he said.

"Did you ever believe in him?"

"Not for a long time," Eric said. "Not since I was fifteen or sixteen."

"You knew he was stealing then?"

"I didn't know that," Eric said. "I knew he couldn't be counted on. At the end of my sophomore year, I found out I was winning an award which was unusual for a sophomore and I asked him to come to the ceremony. Which he didn't do. Later he mentioned business deals and a client who'd arrived unexpectedly and how hard he'd tried to make the ceremony. I knew he was lying and had never intended to come at all." He brushed the hair out of Sarah's eyes. "I'm not very forgiving," he said.

"I just never liked him," Sarah said. "He wasn't interested in me, so I didn't like him. In fact, when I believed in God, I used to pray every night that I'd become a great dancer and that Mother would divorce Daddy."

*   *   *

Their father's attorney stopped Eric in the courtroom after the trial.

"You can see your father," he said.

"Okay?" Sarah asked Eric. "I'll get Rebecca."

Rebecca was standing at the window of the ladies' room when Sarah came in. Next to her the courtroom stenographer was putting on mascara. Rebecca gave Sarah a look of warning.

"I'm not coming out yet," she said.

"We can see Daddy," Sarah said.

Rebecca shook her head.

"No?" Sarah asked.

"I don't want to see him," Rebecca said.

*   *   *

Rebecca rode in the back seat on the drive back to Old Greenwich.

"I warned you," Eric said.

"I thought it was courageous of him to admit it," Sarah said.

"That's why he called me last night," Eric said. "To tell me what he was going to do."

"He seemed relieved," Sarah said.

"Rebec?" Eric asked. "We've been lying for a long time."

But Rebecca simply sat in the back seat with her hands folded, her face impassive, and watched the traffic pass by her side of the car.

* * *

Sarah was practicing for the first time in weeks. She lined up kitchen chairs in the living room for a barre, took the full-length mirror off her mother's door, set it up against the couch and turned on the radio.

"What a privilege," Eric said. "I can study anatomy while you dance."

"You can study anatomy in Mother's room."

"It's full of ghosts."

"Or my room."

"Listen, Sarah," Eric said, "it's very difficult to study anything with the radio on."

"You could go to the library," Sarah said. "I can't practice at the library."

But Eric sat instead in the living room with the radio on and Sarah counting and leaping and arabesquing around his chair.

"I have a headache," he said. "At least turn the music down."

"The trial's over," Sarah said. "You can go back to Cambridge."

* * *

But the fact was that Eric didn't want to go back to Cambridge. He didn't even want to leave the apartment for the library, as if the apartment could take flight in his short absence—or the contents of the apartment and his sisters. That was the truth of it. These precarious months had unbalanced them, as though they'd been walking narrow wires above the crowd, in costume, the four of them, slipping occasionally, one off balance and then the other, one down, flopping like a stuffed doll in the net below. He knew that alone, one or two of them on the wire could not possibly manage without falling.

"I'm worried about Rebecca," Eric said.

Sarah closed her eyes, leaned her head against the back of the couch.

"Me too," she said.

"What would you do if a man you loved betrayed you?"

"Shoot him," Sarah said, getting up from the couch, replacing the mirror. "I might even shoot him if he didn't betray me. I don't like men," she said, gathering her things for dance class, tying her hair back. "Sometimes," she said, putting her shoes and tights and leotard in her dance bag, "I don't even like you."

*   *   *

Rebecca picked Eliza up at the Leuders' at six after she got off work.

"I'm sorry," Mrs. Leuders whispered at the door. "I heard."

"You don't need to whisper," Rebecca said. "Liza knows," she said. "Everyone knows." Mrs. Leuders reached out to touch her shoulder and Rebecca pulled back. She imagined ripping Mrs. Leuders' matching shirt and skirt in small pieces. She imagined pulling her bright blond hair. She rubbed her eyes to cancel her imaginings and took Eliza's hand.

"You promised me," Eliza said. She was crying.

"I promised to take you the third day," Rebecca said. "It was over today. Over, over, over," she said. "There won't be any more days."

"What do you mean?"

"I mean there won't be any more days, you moron."

Eliza pulled her hand away and cried out loud.

"Cry for everyone to hear," Rebecca said. "Let's both cry. Scream. Let's take off our clothes."

Eliza put her hands over her ears.

"I'm sorry," Rebecca said, stopping against a tree, pulling her sister towards her.

"It's just that you promised me and you broke your promise."

"It wasn't a carnival, Liza," Rebecca said. "You didn't miss a thing."

* * *

Sarah was on the bed reading and Eliza climbed up next to her, put her head under her arm.

"Did you ever hate Rebecca?" she asked.

Sarah marked the corner of her book and put it down.

"Sure," Sarah said, "Off and on. How come?"

"Well, I never did," Eliza said. "I thought she was wonderful."

"I hate Rebecca when she's too good to be true."

"She's too bad to be true right now," Eliza said. "Like you used to be. Mean." She narrowed her eyes and looked at herself in the mirror over the bed. "Mean as a snake, mean as an alligator. Mean"—she turned over on her back and stiffened her body—"as Tim Lewis in second grade."

* * *

That night after supper, after the lights were out and Rebecca had read about the mermaid in *Animal Family*, she tried to hold her younger sister, but Eliza resisted, pulled back, moved over into the corner of the bed they had shared since April.

"You're not my mother," she said to Rebecca. "You're not even a very nice sister." In the bathroom, Rebecca looked at herself in the mirror. She should cut her hair, she thought. Shoulder length. She tilted her head so her long hair fell all the way to one side.

"Rebecca." Sarah knocked quietly on the door.

"I'm busy," Rebecca said, but Sarah opened the door anyway, stood in the archway.

"You can't take it out on Liza," Sarah said.

"That's my business."

"She's counted on you ever since this happened."

Rebecca parted her hair in the middle. Then she brushed it.

"She can count on you for a while," she said to Sarah. "You're old enough."

She was glad she'd said that, Rebecca thought to herself when Sarah had left her alone in the bathroom.

Glad to be done with them all, pressing on her life like mongrel dogs. Even Eric. She wished he'd leave for Cambridge tonight.

* * *

Monique has called Sarah three times," Eric said when Rebecca came out of the bathroom.

"Tell Sarah."

"I did," Eric said. "She's locked herself in her room with the usual Walker maturity."

Rebecca kicked the door to their bedroom. "I have to come in," she said to Sarah.

She heard the lock turn.

"You don't have to kick," Sarah said. She was sitting on her bed in a leotard and tights. She'd been crying.

"Is this about Daddy or dancing?" Rebecca asked.

"Neither," Sarah said, and went into the room with Eric. He sat down on the couch beside her.

"Tell me what happened in New York to make you quit dancing?" he asked.

"I wish people would leave me alone," she said.

He leaned against the back of the couch and stretched out his legs. He'd call Gayatri, he thought. Tell her to come to Old Greenwich and get a job in the hospital there with him. She could cook rice meals and hot breads, he thought, remembering the past winter together in Cambridge. She could rub his back if he had insomnia. They'd take the lavender-striped bedroom and sleep in a single bed.

"Eric," Sarah asked quietly, "what do you think about Mother?"

"I think Mother is at the Manor Lodge eating beef Stroganoff and noodles at this moment and making plans for the colors she'll be using for pot holders in evening recreation."

"Be serious," Sarah said. "You know."

"I talked to her doctor this afternoon and he says she's better."

"Much?"

"A little," he said. "It takes a long time."

"I miss her," Sarah said, surprised at her own admission, especially to Eric but even to herself, of this loss.

Rebecca locked the door to her mother's room, turned on the light and undressed. Naked, she stood in front of the mirror and examined herself. She had never looked at herself absolutely naked before. She wasn't plump but thick with large thighs and flesh around her belly. Her breasts were high and small, and from the side there were small hills where her weight settled. She presumed a man would find that provocative. A man had never seen her naked before. She had been kissed by Tommy Otis, Johnny Flanders and Carson Falk, and been touched by Johnny Flanders on the side of her breasts as he kissed her, but that was fully clothed. She had a reputation for being old-fashioned, which she had expected to discard in college. She had dreamed of lying naked with a boy. She had dreamed of more than that, but she hadn't expected to act on her dreams until some distant moment she couldn't imagine. And then today, after her father's trial, working at the prescription counter at Aikens' Drugs, Michael Ryan came in with a prescription for penicillin, and she'd said they ought to get together sometime about Yale and he'd said tomorrow if he was over the flu. The whole rest of the afternoon she made astonishing plans in her head with Mike Ryan. She couldn't wait to get home to see how she looked naked in the mirror in her mother's room.

"Telephone," Eric said, banging on the door.

"Take a message," she said and dressed quickly.

*　*　*

"It was Johnny Barber," Eric said when she came out of the bedroom.

"What did he want?" she asked.

"He wanted you to go to a party tomorrow."

"I'm busy," she said.

"Good," Eric said. "You're probably the fourteenth girl he's called."

"Too bad for Johnny Barber," Rebecca said, stretching, assuming an unfamiliar and suggestive pose. "Because I'm thinking of sleeping with everyone I see."

"Splendid, Rebec," Eric said, crawling into his sleeping bag. "What a first-rate idea."

14

Rebecca was first aware of trouble at the Fourth of July picnic at the beach. Not ordinary trouble either, but real danger, as though she were swimming in an unpredictable current with sudden drops where people were commonly known to have drowned.

"I'm getting overtired," Eric had said to her one night when she'd come home late as usual.

"Then sleep," Rebecca said, going straight to the bedroom and dressing in the dark.

"It's difficult to sleep imagining what you might be doing until three o'clock in the morning," Eric said, leaning against the door frame.

"I haven't been in trouble," she said.

"The fact is you're in trouble already."

Rebecca climbed into her bed, which she had to herself again since Eliza had moved to her own bed.

"Since you turned mean," Eliza said to her one night, and Rebecca did not argue.

"Have you considered a shrink?" Eric asked. "I think you need someone to talk to."

"I'm talking to you perfectly well," she said, pulling a sheet over her. "We speak in English and our conversation makes perfect sense."

"I'm not saying you've flipped," Eric said, sitting down next to her. "I think it's been more difficult for you to face what Daddy did."

"Shut up." She turned away from him to the wall.

"I think you're in trouble, Bec."

She knew she was in trouble as she sat on the beach at two in the morning after the Fourth of July picnic with Billy Thrower's head in her lap. She'd known it for weeks. Out every night with someone— Michael Ryan and Tommy Power and Dick Stokes and Derek May. "Nice boys," her mother would say. "Dependable. From good families who have been in Old Greenwich for years."

Rebecca had a reputation for caution and reserve.

"Straight arrow," Eric would say.

"Sensible," Rebecca replied. "Old Greenwich is too small for romances. Besides, I remember most of the boys here when they were in grade school with runny noses and bad breath."

She went to the parties but was unwilling to lose herself in the madness of being in the wake of growing up, for madness was exactly what it seemed.

"Don't you ever get bored?" Eric asked her once. "Moderation isn't exactly the spice of life."

"Listen, Eric, this family needs someone who isn't prone to cardiac arrest."

She had many friends among the boys in her class, a few of whom interested her in a way that predicted a relationship, but she withdrew, not in any absolute way, but to the extent that no one with whom she spent time was allowed to be close to her.

"Sometimes you're a creep," Johnny Barber had told her once.

"I know," Rebecca said. "Maybe when I'm older." She had come to understand that it wasn't so much her privacy that she guarded but herself, as though she was fearful of being overwhelmed. It was sexual, certainly, a fear of her own desire, of where it would take her, so she appeared to be a young woman of surprising self-containment, which was false.

"Unapproachable," Eric said.

"Not like Sarah," Rebecca said.

"Worse," Eric said, "because you appear to be warm and then fade away."

And then two weeks ago, Billy Thrower came by Aikens' Drugs while she was working and asked her out with the New Canaan crowd, an older group who had jobs at eighteen and didn't go to college, who raced their cars on Saturday nights on the freeway and drank too much while they were still in high school. They married young and grew fat before their thirties.

"Billy Thrower has a terrible reputation," Sarah said one night, waiting up for Rebecca to come in.

"He's very nice," she said. "You all are snobs," she said. "He's poor, that's all. He hasn't had advantages like us, Sarah Walker. You may as well get used to it. His parents can't afford to send him to college."

131

"Are you still a virgin?" Sarah asked after their lights were out.

"Of course," Rebecca replied coolly.

* * *

Rebecca had difficulty sleeping. If she closed her eyes, Edward Walker appeared on the inside lids, and she couldn't get rid of him. She didn't have conversations with him as she used to have or imagine caring for him, cooking his breakfast, brushing the lint off his gray suit as she used to do. She didn't dream about him. But when he materialized as a very small replica of Edward Walker seated in the corner of her brain, she couldn't get rid of him without opening her eyes and watching the car headlights skip past her window.

One night in desperation Sarah asked, "Can you imagine how disappointed Daddy would be to know you're going out with Billy Thrower?"

She didn't reply, but she had thought about that. And to her surprise and confusion, she wanted her father to know.

* * *

She had begun to wear makeup, purple lipstick from Aikens' and blush. She grew her nails.

Once she asked Darcy Maxwell, who worked behind the cosmetics counter, about birth control pills.

"You need them?" Darcy asked, snapping her fingers at Rebecca, raising her brown-penciled eyelids.

Rebecca shrugged.

"How old are you, anyway?" Darcy asked.

"Eighteen," Rebecca said. "I go to college in September."

"Well," Darcy said confidentially, "I was only fifteen or sixteen when it happened first. Like, it's no big deal."

* * *

"Come on, Rebecca," Billy Thrower said. He lifted her skirt and kissed her belly.

"Nope," she said.

He pressed his head against her and closed his eyes.

When she got up, he grabbed her ankle and pulled her down on her back against the cold damp sand. He had been drinking too much to be effective, and she rolled away from him.

"How come, Rebecca?"

"I'm not ready," she said, shaking out her blanket, wrapping it around her like a shawl.

"How long does it take for you to be ready?" Billy Thrower asked, turning over on his back, grabbing her arm. "I'm getting old waiting for you." He banged his fist against the sand. "Promises," he said. "You're full of promises."

It was a clear night with stars, and she could see him half sleeping on the blanket next to her, lifting his head occasionally and dropping off to sleep. In the distance she could still hear firecrackers from the backyards of private homes. None on the beach. The beach had closed at midnight. The rest of the New

133

Canaan crowd had left then, off with their girls to the backs of cars or living rooms with the lights out.

"Have a good time, Billy," they shouted.

At first they'd kissed lying on one blanket with the other blanket covering their backs.

"Please," he'd whispered in her ear, and she was aware of wanting Billy Thrower. But not enough. Not enough to undress, as he'd suggested at first, or even, she discovered to her surprise, to let him touch her underneath her shirt.

"Jeez, Rebecca," he'd said, sitting up, drinking orange juice and vodka from a thermos. "What do you want?"

"I don't know," she'd said, wrapping her blanket around her back to keep out the sea chill.

"That, my princess, is clear as a bell."

Often when she lay with Billy Thrower, she'd make believe they were in the study of their old house, the Clauses' house on the Sound. It was very late, three or four in the morning, and upstairs her parents were supposed to be sleeping. Dreaming like this, she'd be barely conscious of Billy Thrower's hand on her thigh, on the back of her neck. She'd imagine her father waking, putting on his robe. She'd pretend to hear him coming down the steps, turning on the hall light. And still she'd lie on the couch with Billy Thrower in her daydream, her back to the imagined presence of her father as he found them lying together.

* * *

Gayatri moved in at the end of June and took over the lavender-striped bedroom with Eric.

"Can't we keep this in the family?" Sarah complained to Eric.

"She may be in the family," Eric said.

"I doubt it," Sarah said. "In the end she'll choose to marry a healthy man."

"Listen, Sarah," Eric said, "I need her. I'm under terrific strain."

Gayatri was a quiet, sweet and dutiful woman with gentle and unobtrusive ways. Unless there was work to be done or she was at the hospital, she stayed in her bedroom studying, out of the way.

"It drives me crazy," Rebecca said. "She's so good, I'd like to smother her."

"It's necessary for Eliza to have someone around since you've become so busy," Eric said.

"What about Sarah?"

"What about Sarah? She needs a mother as much as Liza."

"So do I," Rebecca snapped and shut herself in the bathroom.

* * *

"We've got to be nice about Gayatri," Eliza said one night to Sarah after the lights were out. "She may leave."

"A terrific idea."

"Then Eric will leave," Eliza said.

"Even better," Sarah said from her bed, where she was practicing raising her legs up over her head.

135

"Then who will take care of us?" Eliza asked. "Rebecca's never home anymore."

"Me," Sarah said. "I'll be all that's left."

* * *

After Gayatri came, Eric was sick all the time. He went to work at the hospital in Greenwich where both he and Gayatri had summer research jobs, but if he was home he slept on the couch, propped up by pillows, covered lightly in sheets. He suffered from shortness of breath and pains in the back of his neck. He had stomach cramps and headaches, which could, he explained, be related to a spinal disease he had been treating another patient for. Gayatri made tea for him and small cakes. She rubbed his neck and the small of his back. She made his bed with fresh sheets and served him special dinners. Often at night she read to him.

"If Eric doesn't leave," Sarah said, "then I will."

"You tried that once," Rebecca said, "and it didn't work out."

"I'll go to Salem, Illinois, this time, or Nebraska," she said. "Not New York."

In fact, Monique called Rebecca to say that the Ballet Theatre would offer Sarah a scholarship. She could go to school in New York and come home weekends.

"It's what you always wanted," Rebecca said.

"She doesn't give up," Sarah said.

Sarah was practicing again daily as she used to practice, hour after hour of routine and exercise, but the practice was different than it had been before New York, without imagination.

* * *

Alicia Walker was given permission to have one visitor, and she asked to see Sarah.

"Not me?" Rebecca asked.

"She asked about you, Rebec," Eric said from his place on the couch. "But she can only see one of us."

"How come it was Sarah?"

"She probably thinks you don't need her as much," Eric said. "Poor fool."

Sarah spent all day dressing. She tied her hair up in a chignon and down loose around her face. She tried pants and a jacket, jeans and a shirt, a dress, a skirt and blouse, settling finally on a dress that made her look very young, with a yoke collar and loose waist, her hair down and pulled back in a ribbon.

"You look like a little girl," Eric said.

On the train which she took to the town nearest Manor Lodge, Sarah felt like a young girl, like she had felt when she was very young, five or six, and she had waited after school for her mother to pick her up. Seeing Alicia Walker come up the school driveway looking beautiful, Sarah had jumped up in wonderful anticipation of holding her mother's hand, of walking down Main Street with her. She remembered nights then, after the light was out, after her story, when Alicia Walker would sit beside Sarah on her bed and Sarah leaned her head against the soft silk of her mother's gown, smelled the faint mustiness of flowers from the talcum her mother used after her bath.

Sometimes at night, waiting for Rebecca to come in with Billy Thrower, Sarah put herself to sleep with the memory of her mother beside her.

Alicia Walker was dressed in a yellow flowered dress and sandals, her cheeks were flushed with sunlight, her eyes serene after weeks of separation from troubles. And seeing Alicia like that, the night-time memory of her mother when she was a child, Sarah wept.

"I'm sorry," she whispered into the soft shoulder of Alicia Walker's dress. "I have missed you so much."

* * *

The apartment was dark, but Eric was sitting up on the couch and smoking when Rebecca came home on the Fourth of July.

"Do you know what time it is?"

"Four-fifteen," Rebecca said. "I saw it on the church clock."

"You've been to church, then."

"Where else?" Rebecca said. "What are you doing up?"

"Sarah went to see Mother today, and the rest of us have been to see Dad," Eric said, turning on the light beside the couch.

Rebecca dropped the blankets, still sandy, on the couch.

"So?"

"So I expected you'd at least go on a holiday."

"I told you I don't intend to go at all," Rebecca said. "Holiday or not."

"Too busy upholding the Walkers' honorable name?" Eric said, taking her gently by the shoulders. "Listen, Rebecca," he began quietly, but she had pulled back by then and punched him on the shoulder with her closed fist.

15

Alicia Walker's physician came to the apartment above Aikens' Drugs the first Sunday in August during the longest unbroken heat wave in Connecticut since 1938. No one was dressed. Sarah lay face down on her bed, wrapped in a wet towel.

"You could get bone chill," Eric said from the couch.

"Good," Sarah moaned.

Rebecca was in the bathroom trying on eye shadow in different shades while Eliza, sitting on the closed toilet seat, watched her.

"I don't like shiny green on you," she said.

"I do," Rebecca said, raising her eyebrows. "It's my best color."

"It looks cheap," Eliza said, resting her chin on the sink.

"Who told you that word?" Rebecca asked.

"I know it," Eliza said. "I use it all the time."

"Sure," Rebecca said and walked into the flowered

bedroom with one eye dull blue and one iridescent green.

"Did you tell Eliza I look cheap?"

"Probably," Sarah said. "Although I thought I said tacky."

"It's too hot for conversation," Eric called from the couch.

"This isn't a conversation," Rebecca said.

"It's an argument," Sarah said.

"It's a fight," Rebecca said.

"Don't fight," Eliza said. "I didn't mean cheap. Sarah's right. She said tacky . . ."

Which is when Dr. Mancari knocked on the living room door and Rebecca answered it.

Eric said he was too sick to get up and would Gayatri bring him pillows. Eliza came in and sat on Eric's feet. Rebecca put on a sundress, but didn't bother to wash her face.

"Welcome to the traveling circus," Eric said to Dr. Mancari with a weak gesture around the room to include the family. "Presently grounded due to the heat. I apologize for Rebecca, who was just practicing her clown act."

Dr. Mancari had come about Alicia, who was much better, he promised, nearly well in fact. She dressed for supper now and worked in rehabilitation every day. She had gone to church in the village regularly and to a party given by a resident doctor. She spoke easily and asked about all of them, which she hadn't been able to do at first. She cried after Sarah visited her, he said, and that was a very good sign because she hadn't been able to cry for years. There had been no lapses since the end of June, and it was quite possible that she'd be home by the first of September.

He had made a special trip to talk to them because he thought it wise for the Walker children to find a house, an economical one. There was money for a small rent.

"Certainly," Eric agreed. "It would make a difference if she didn't have to come home to this."

Rebecca walked Dr. Mancari to the door when he left, walked with him down the street to his car.

"A house would be better," Dr. Mancari said. "It's difficult for your mother, who grew up in this town, to live in a place over the drugstore. She is a woman whose sense of self is related to her surroundings, which is why the house on the Sound was so important to her."

"Sometimes I guess that it was more difficult for Mother to lose that house than Daddy."

Dr. Mancari opened the door to his car and sat down in the driver's seat.

"I understand that you've been wonderful, Rebecca," he said. "All of you children."

"No," she said. "Not really." She wanted to tell him what she had been doing. She wanted to tell someone, but he knew her as the caretaker. He might not allow Alicia to come home if he knew Rebecca was splintering like rotted wood.

"You know about Yale?" she asked just before he pulled away.

"That you're going in the fall. I think it's marvelous. Your mother is very proud of you."

"Perhaps I should stay home," she said. It was automatic. She had not in a conscious way considered that possibility.

"I didn't know it was a question," he said.

"I mean, if Mother needs me, I could stay home next semester, the whole year in fact," she said. "I don't have to go in September."

"I suppose you could," he said softly, brushing his fingers through his thin gray hair, wiping the perspiration from his forehead.

"You want an answer, don't you?" He touched her fingers, which held the car door, held his own hand on top of hers. "But it's not my question," he said.

"I know," she said, disappointed, obviously disappointed by the fall of her face, by the urgency with which she tried to hold this man through conversation. "It's my question." She found her mind racing for more conversation. "I just don't know," she said.

"It's not Yale," he said to her gently in a voice that was both comforting and strong. "It's more than that you want an answer to from me." With unusual care, he took her hand off the door to the car. "But whether you stay next year to help your mother or not is a decision you have to make."

He didn't hesitate. He started the car engine, waved to her gaily, as though they'd been having a pleasant talk, and drove off.

Later that afternoon she looked up Dr. Mancari in the telephone directory and found a Dr. Anthony

Mancari listed in Cos Cob, but when she called, a woman, probably his wife, answered the phone, and she hung up without speaking.

It was her day off, and she was tired from days and days of working at a tedious job, from lying too late every night with Billy Thrower, from the slow drain the last months had had on her life. She lay in bed in the dusty hot sun, the room thick and oppressive, rancid with the lingering odor of food in a place without breeze, and slept off and on, as though drunk or drugged, aware of her surroundings as a sick person is aware of objects obstructed floating in and out of view.

When she got up that afternoon, still heavy with sleep, not rested but not so anxious as she had been with Dr. Mancari, she had made up her mind about Yale. In fact, it wasn't an intellectual decision. It had come to her in that hot room, half sleeping, like the furniture had come, wandering in and out of vision, until in her dream she simply saw herself at home and not at Yale. She saw them living in a small house in Old Greenwich, as though the decision of staying home next year had not been hers to make but had been made for her some time ago and simply hadn't advanced itself until now.

"I've decided to take off a semester at least and stay home with Mother," she told Eric when she got up.

"Martyred decision?" Eric asked.

She hesitated. "Nope," she said. "I don't think so.

I think"—she sat down next to him so Gayatri or Sarah wouldn't hear—"I think it's for me I'm staying home."

"For you to do what?"

"I'm not sure," she said. "Maybe to settle. It wouldn't have made much sense to go to Yale and explode."

"Is that how you feel?" Eric asked, taking one of her wrists in his hand.

"I don't feel well," she said.

Which is what she finally told Dr. Mancari when she called him on the phone later and got him on the first ring.

"If you need to see a doctor, I can make arrangements," he said to her.

"I want to see you," she said boldly.

"I know several doctors who specialize in people your age," he began.

"Adolescents," she said fiercely. "As though it were a disease."

It gave her a sense of victory to hang up the phone before he had a chance to speak again.

"Looking for fathers?" Eric asked her after she hung up, but he asked it gently and Rebecca wasn't upset.

"I suppose," she said.

In the bathroom, she emptied the makeup in the sink. With purple lipstick, she made flowers on her forehead and her cheeks. She rubbed green iridescent eye shadow in stripes across her face and painted her ears with pink blush. On her chest, just at the top of the round neck of her tee shirt, she made a huge heart and colored it in.

"I'm sorry the good doctor didn't have a chance to see your getup," Eric said from the couch. "What an opportunity for a man of his talents."

"Becky." Eliza laughed, half laughed, and then she stopped. "Are you playing?"

"I'm perfectly serious," Rebecca said and sat down.

"You're not going out like that, are you?" Eliza said.

"I'm sorry about Yale," Eric said. "And everything else," he added, sensing her disappointment as though it were living silica in the dense room.

"It's fine. *Fine*," Rebecca said, crossing her legs, staring out the window at Main Street. "Please," she said, her voice breaking, "don't talk to me."

* * *

Rebecca called Patty Miller after Eric was asleep. "We need a house for Mother to come home to," she said brusquely, embarrassed to ask for help. "The apartment over Aikens' depressed her."

"Of course," Patty said enthusiastically. "Poor girl. Of course she needs a house."

"A small house," Rebecca went on, not anxious to be involved in conversation. "And inexpensive."

"I think I can find one just perfect for you," Patty said. "There's a colonial for rent on Talbot."

"Maybe close to the Sound," Rebecca said, "if possible."

When Patty started on the advantages of brick over

frame and floor plans, the cost of heat without storm windows, Rebecca excused herself to read to Liza.

"Just a regular house," she said in closing, "if you happen to hear of one."

* * *

Eric had been in bed since the beginning of the heat wave, which still in the middle of August showed no signs of relief. Gayatri had taken over, inspired by the heat, alive in it, cleaning the apartment, cooking and cooking in the tiny kitchen, so the smells of food crept into the furthest corners of the room, washing curtains and clothes.

"Have you seen this?" Rebecca said to Sarah one morning before she left for work. Sarah stood beside her sister and watched Gayatri in the living room with a tub of water, washing Eric's hands and face, folding the sheet back over his body.

"For chrissake," Rebecca said aloud, but Gayatri shushed her from the living room. Eliza finally asked if he was dying.

"Of boredom," Rebecca said. "And motherly affection."

The Greenwich Hospital said his contract for the summer would be terminated if he missed any more time.

"She has to leave," Sarah said of Gayatri. "She's killing Eric."

"There is nothing the matter with you," Rebecca said to him one afternoon. "You're fine." But Eric simply turned his face away. He wasn't even funny any longer.

147

* * *

Sarah visited Edward Walker regularly, twice a week on Tuesdays and Thursdays. Occasionally she took Eliza, and the three of them, even Sarah and her father, talked more easily than they had ever talked before, as though his admission of failure had eliminated familiar barriers. She wanted to tell him that one afternoon, but he brought it up himself because he had written a letter to Rebecca and was, he said, thinking of the differences in his daughters.

"Is it a personal letter?" Sarah asked, putting the letter in her dance bag.

"I've asked her to visit," her father said.

He looked better than he had in the trial, younger, and on the days that Sarah came to visit he dressed for the occasion.

"I read a lot," he told Sarah. "And think, of course. There's no point in looking back."

"What will you do when you get out?"

"I don't know," he said. "Work at something, but that will be difficult, of course. I'm not a bargain as an accountant at the moment."

Sarah read the letter and put it in her dance bag.

"Rebecca won't come," she said.

"Perhaps not," Edward Walker said, and she could tell he was anxious about it.

"She doesn't even want to talk about you."

She thought of telling her father about the boys from New Canaan, about Billy Thrower and how he brought Rebecca home close to dawn many nights.

"She's changed," Sarah said. "She wears makeup."

148

"Things could be worse," Edward Walker said.

They are, she wanted to say. *They're terrible.* But instead she told her father that things were going well except for Eric, who would recover if Gayatri returned to Cambridge.

"Does Rebecca ever ask how I am when you come back from these visits?" he interrupted.

"Usually she's working when I come back," Sarah said, evading the question. "I don't see her for hours."

"I suppose she forgets you've been here," he said.

*   *   *

"I forgave Daddy when he admitted he'd embezzled," Sarah said simply to Eric when she came home that afternoon. She gave Eric the letter to give to Rebecca. "It's Mother's illness that upsets me."

"Don't mention Mother," Eric snapped, "and for chrissake, don't cry."

Gayatri came through the kitchen with tea and sat down next to Eric.

"When the heat breaks"—she smiled at Sarah— "your brother will be better."

"What will happen to you if he is well?" Sarah said with vengeance.

But Gayatri, smiling, sipping her tea, did not seem to understand.

*   *   *

Monique called Rebecca that evening to say that she wanted to take Sarah with her for the weekend to see the performances and meet with the director of the Ballet Theatre.

"Do you want to go?" Rebecca asked flatly.

149

Sarah shook her head.

"Another time," Rebecca said into the phone.

* * *

The next morning Sarah and Rebecca lay in bed and listened to the steady rain against the windows, the splash of cars in the street, the high singsong of Gayatri's voice from the living room to the kitchen, like a jungle bird: "*T-whee, t-whee.*" "Coming, Eric." "There, Eric." "Now, now, Eric." "Better sleep, Eric." "Breakfast, Liza." "Up, up, up, girls." "Breakfast now." "Dinner, dinner" "*T-whee.*" And the low groan of Eric from the couch: "Ga-ya-tri. *Ga-ya-tri.*"

"Let's get rid of Gayatri," Sarah said. Rebecca looked over at her younger sister, who lay on her back with her legs perpendicular to her body, looking very much like Sarah the dancer, but reminding her in the pitch of excitement in her voice of Sarah when they were both very young—of waking in the morning to Sarah in the next bed saying, "Let's do something."

"Let's," Rebecca said.

Later that day Rebecca opened the letter from her father.

"Come," it said, and underneath was a picture he had drawn of a square-faced man in glasses with turned-down lips. She put it away in her top drawer.

16

First Sarah and Rebecca short-sheeted the bed in the lavender-striped bedroom where Gayatri slept. They folded the sheet in half so Gayatri's feet would stop halfway down; in the cup made by the halved sheet, they put a bowlful of cooked spaghetti noodles.

Rebecca was out with Billy Thrower until late, but Sarah was there in the living room with Eric when Gayatri screamed and came in carrying a small handful of wet spaghetti noodles.

"A joke?" She smiled feebly, holding the noodles up to Sarah.

"I don't know what you're talking about," Sarah replied.

"In my bed?"

"Maybe Eric did it," Sarah said.

"Very funny," Eric said. "Very goddamned funny."

He got up from the couch and followed Gayatri into the bedroom. Sarah watched them carry the wet spaghetti noodles to the kitchen, take out a clean sheet and remake the bed. When Eric came back to the living room to get his blanket, he didn't speak.

Sarah was still up when Rebecca came home.

"Did it work?" Rebecca asked.

"Eric's furious," Sarah said.

"It was a very cute joke," Gayatri said at the breakfast table in her careful English. "I have never had that joke done."

"I would have killed you if I were her," Eric said after Gayatri left for the market.

"You're too weak for extreme measures, Eric," Rebecca said. "The point is that it's a bad idea to have her here."

"She's better behaved than any of you," Eric said.

"She's beautifully behaved," Rebecca said. "That's the trouble. I feel like a harlot in a class A hotel."

"I couldn't manage without her, Rebecca."

Rebecca cleaned the breakfast dishes and piled them in the sink, wiped off the table. "Maybe if you had to take care of yourself for a change . . ." She gathered her things to leave for work.

"Shut up," he said, back on the couch again, thumbing through medical books. "At least Gayatri is intelligent, which is more than I can say for your mating choices."

* * *

Sarah had a recital in New Haven the first weekend in September in which she had a major role. Most days she was gone all day, and it seemed to Rebecca that her sister was back to her old disciplined self, only gentler than she'd been before Alicia's breakdown. So she was surprised one afternoon at work to get a call from Sarah's regular dance teacher in New Haven saying that Sarah was doing very poorly.

*   *   *

"Let's get married," Rebecca said to Billy Thrower, lying on the beach that night, watching the stars in a black sky.

"Are you kidding?"

"My family's driving me crazy," she said.

"Mine's no picnic," Billy said. "Like, take my father, for example."

"The point is if we get married we don't live with either family. Right?"

Billy rolled over on his stomach. He threw one leg across Rebecca.

"Are you kidding?" He kissed her open mouth. "I mean, I don't really want to get married," he said, and kissed her again, pulled his body on top of hers. "What I want . . ."

"You're too heavy," Rebecca said, squirming beneath him.

"For crissake, girl, what do you want?"

She turned over on her stomach and put her head in her hands.

"I don't know," she said. "I honestly don't know."

"Someday you're going to drive a guy nuts, and he won't be a sweet-natured guy like me and put up with this messing around like a couple of ten-year-olds."

"Death by drowning," Rebecca said. "That's what I want."

153

"Very good. Death by drowning. What a super idea." He stretched out on the sand. "I don't like messing around with smart girls. It gives me a headache."

* * *

"What do you know about Monique?" Eric asked when Rebecca came home from work the last week before Sarah's recital.

"Nothing. Absolutely nothing," Rebecca said.

"Sarah came home at lunch today and said she wouldn't rehearse. She said if anyone called, say she'd gone to Nebraska." Eric was sitting up and Gayatri was cutting his hair. He was dressed for the first time in two days, in blue jeans and a pajama top.

"See?" Gayatri said, smiling. "Now it's cool again, your brother is much better. I cut his hair and he'll be fine."

"Like Sampson," Rebecca said, collapsing in the chair. "Did the dance teacher call?"

"Yes, she called and called and so did her assistant. It's been a regular social center here at the Walkers'. She's coming over."

"Now?"

"Soon."

"I can hardly wait," Rebecca said. "Company. Bring out the silver. Where's Sarah?"

"Packing." He looked at himself in the mirror. "Not too short," he cautioned Gayatri.

"Packing?" she asked. "For Nebraska?"

"She's going to Dockertys' to spend the night. And she tells me she's quitting dance."

Rebecca went into the bedroom and watched Sarah pack.

"Are you going for long?"

"I'm going until that dance teacher leaves me alone," she said.

"What does she want?" Rebecca asked.

"Me," Sarah said. "As though I'm made of styrofoam."

Rebecca changed to shorts to meet Billy at the beach.

"She wants me to go to New York to dance," Sarah said. "She won't leave me alone about it. I hate her."

Rebecca put her arm on Sarah's. "Tell her to go away," she said.

"I can't," Sarah said.

"Are you afraid of her?"

"I don't know what I'm afraid of."

Rebecca went over to the mirror and brushed her hair, pulling it back off her face.

"Rebec," Sarah said, "I can't dance now. I'm just not good."

"How come?"

"This year probably. Mother and stuff," she said. "It'll come back, but I can't be pushed."

* * *

Monique sat across from Eric. "Curry," she said, sniffing. "You must be cooking curry." She smiled at Gayatri, who brought in a tray of tea and slender Indian cookies.

"Sarah has been under too much pressure this year to think of going to New York."

"She's very good," the dance teacher said. "She could be great," she said. She was a thin, artificial woman who seemed nearly real, made of quality plastic. During the time she sat in the Walkers' living room, she moved only once and that was to gesture in Eric's direction. It was a gesture so perfect it seemed made up.

"She's not going to New York," Eric said simply.

He listened to the woman tell him of Sarah's special talent, of her need at this moment to be in the best situation for dance, of her beauty and grace, and finally, violating the Walkers' insistent privacy, she said, "Sarah desperately needs a mother."

"Sarah has a mother," Rebecca said fiercely.

And Eric, in a surprising move, got up from the couch where he was half lying in his blue jeans and pajama top, took the woman by the arm to the door, and she moved with him, unresisting, as though it had been choreographed in advance.

"Leave us alone," he said.

*　*　*

"Jesus," Rebecca said after she had gone.

"I think she wants to take ownership of Sarah, as if she were up for sale," he said. "Scary."

"I'll say," Rebecca said.

*　*　*

The next attack against Gayatri was silence.

"Not a word," Sarah said.

"I think it's awful," Eliza said, so they arranged for Liza to stay at the Leuders' until Gayatri left.

156

"It's not that we don't like Gayatri," Rebecca said, walking Eliza to the Leuders'. "It's just that Eric will stay in bed forever if she doesn't stop nursing him."

Eliza was not persuaded.

"It's the silent act," Eric said to Gayatri at the table. Neither Sarah nor Rebecca had spoken for several hours. "One of the least-used acts in this particular family circus," he said.

The silence made Gayatri sing. At first quietly under her breath while the carrot soup was served, and then to deter the silence she sang louder, like a frightened bird, during the main course.

"Would you stop the singing?" Eric asked. "Please. My nerves are on edge this evening."

"Oh, sorry, sorry," she said quietly. "I didn't mean to." But during dessert, she was humming under her breath. Eric got up from the table and went to the lavender-striped bedroom.

"I hate music at the table," he said.

Rebecca and Sarah cleared the table in silence and did the dishes.

"Oh, I'll do them," Gayatri said, but getting no response except the clatter of dishes as Sarah and Rebecca went about their work, she went into the lavender-striped bedroom where Eric was and shut the door.

Sarah and Rebecca heard conversation and Eric came out. He stood in the kitchen door and watched them.

"I dislike women," he said finally. "I don't know

why I never realized it until this evening."

Sarah and Rebecca finished the dishes and went to their room.

Eric knocked on the door. "I'm going back to Cambridge tomorrow," he said. "In case either of you is interested."

In the morning when Sarah and Rebecca got up, Gayatri's suitcases were packed by the front door, and Eric, in his pajama top and blue jeans, was making pancakes.

"Is she angry?" Rebecca asked Eric later.

"She's been brought up by a civilized family in a country which has endured generations of fools." He finished the dishes, went in his bedroom and put on a regular shirt for the first time in weeks.

"You said last night you were going back to Cambridge," Rebecca said.

"I thought you were sleeping," Eric said, preparing to go out.

"Where are you going?" Rebecca asked, following him down the back steps and onto Main Street.

"To Bridgeport," he said, "to see Dad."

17

Rebecca couldn't sleep at night. There was a feeling of change around her, of autumn anticipating red on the dark side of maple trees, of cold nights immediately after the sun went down, of friends she had known all of her life, in grammar school, at Christ Church, at tennis camp and beach parties, packing in their bedrooms, packing new clothes to go off in late September. It was as though the days spilled her out on the same side she'd begun them, as though they were revolving doors, throwing her back uncaught.

Michael Ryan kissed her at the last high school party, and that was all.

"For chrissake, Rebecca," Eric said. "Don't be maudlin." He pulled her hair playfully. "Michael Ryan was worth biting in the neck a short time ago."

"I can't help it," Rebecca said.

Eric was cleaning the house, washing the woodwork even, full of purpose since Gayatri had left.

"Other people kissed me," she said quietly. She

was flung across the couch, lying on her stomach.

"Kissable Becky Walker, a regular at the Old Greenwich parties," Eric said.

"Don't." She covered her eyes with her hands.

Missy Clover told Rebecca that she had a bad reputation. "As a friend," she insisted.

"I know," Rebecca said.

"Because of Billy Thrower."

"Of course," Rebecca said and said it boldly, as though a bad reputation was just what she had planned for the summer of her eighteenth year.

She went home with Johnny Barber to the recreation room of his house and lay beside him on the couch.

"It's weird," he said.

"What?" She turned her pelvis towards him and put her hand under his shirt.

"We could have been together for the past two years," he said, "and now all of a sudden it's the end, sort of, and you come up to me," he fumbled.

"Don't talk," she said and kissed him. She had learned to kiss from the boys from New Canaan. She felt Johnny Barber thicken against her thigh and took off her shirt, tossing it behind her, and then she took his face in her hands and kissed him gently.

"Jesus," he whispered. "Jesus . . ."

When Mr. Barber came downstairs looking for Johnny without warning and turned on the light, he found Rebecca lying on the couch in shorts without a shirt.

"Dress," he said.

She couldn't find her shirt. She must have thrown it under something. Johnny jumped up and stood beside his father, lining himself up just behind him so his father couldn't look at him, could look only at Rebecca scrambling on the floor after her shirt. They stood speechless while she looked under the couch, under the couch seats, behind the couch, across the room in case she'd just thrown it and forgotten that, before Johnny finally mumbled something about a wicker chair and she found the yellow knit shirt tossed on the seat of it. The iridescent light of the recreation room made her naked breasts seem four times their normal size, fleshy as summer cantaloupes.

"I have to go," she said as though it was an independent decision.

Mr. Barber took her without Johnny. They drove in silence down Main Street, and he stopped in front of Aikens' Drugs and waited until she went upstairs. She saw his car pull away after she went in the living room.

Eric was waiting up. She crumpled into a chair, buried her head in her arms.

"I want to die," she said.

"I can recommend several possibilities," Eric said lightly, but he got up from the couch and ruffled her hair with his hand, holding it on the top of her head for so long she almost gave in to his touch and told him what had been going on.

Eric was aware that sometime in these last few days he had taken over, as though his mind, like the body's other organs, was regenerative—which in fact

161

he knew, as a doctor, it was; new cells with a fresh vision—but this day, this evening at least, he felt unencumbered with the memory of old cells.

As a young boy, when the pressures of school had been too great, particularly the pressures to be an athlete, which he hadn't the chance of becoming, he went to bed.

"Sick," he'd tell his mother.

She'd sit down beside him on the bed.

"How sick?" She'd feel his head. "You don't feel sick," she'd say.

"Everywhere," he'd say. "All over."

And she'd rub his back, run her fingers through his hair, bring him juices and tea as though he really was sick, although they both knew the illness was not specific but that his mind simply needed time to restore itself.

In high school he was never sick, and even in college except once in retaliation when a girl at Wellesley turned him down. But when he went to medical school and discovered specifically the dangers to his living, he was certain he was subject to every disease mentioned in the texts. He knew, however, that these last two weeks of illness had been in self-defense, to buy time, because inevitably he and Rebecca would have to run the family, in spite of what might happen to Alicia and Edward. He needed the energy for that.

"I hope sometime this year after I go back to school you'll decide to see Dad," Eric said that night before Rebecca went to bed.

"Nope," she said. "Well, maybe. Who knows? Remember when you told me you hated him?"

Eric followed Rebecca into the kitchen, and she made lemonade.

"I don't any longer," he said.

"How come?" she asked, carefully pouring herself a glass of lemonade and Eric one.

He sat down on the kitchen stool, took off his glasses, and rubbed the bridge of his nose marked with the prongs of his glasses.

"Maybe it's a question of understanding," he said. "He did what he did for Mother, to impress her, I suppose, because he was a poor boy from Brooklyn and probably because she required it."

"Stealing?" Rebecca said crossly.

"She had always been taken care of too well," Eric said, finishing the lemonade. "Dad got caught in a maze of dishonesty and couldn't get out, but initially the first lie had been for her. It was wrong and stupid and we all paid for it, but I can't hate him, because I understand it."

"Well, I don't," Rebecca said, picking up her brother's glasses and putting them on so objects in the kitchen melted together without distinguishing shapes, only colors, and those faded as though they'd been filtered through a gray lens. "Yik," she said, taking the glasses off. "I hate what your glasses do to my eyes."

"I think it's a man's fantasy, trying to please a woman like that. Or at least a man who grew up at the time Dad did," Eric said. "Besides," he said, "your relationship with him has always been different."

"And it's over," Rebecca said.

That night she had waking dreams of the New Haven–Hartford local running Edward Walker down as he walked across the tracks.

* * *

Rebecca was in trouble with the group from New Canaan, especially Micky Olman.

"Rich kid," he had said to her.

"Oh, sure," she'd said. "Very rich."

There was a challenge in the tone of his voice and unaccountable curiosity as well. If there was a leader of the group, it was Micky. He was quieter than the rest, and they invariably waited for his decision, even a small decision, before taking action.

"Like, let's go to McDonald's," Billy Thrower would say. "What do you think, Micky?"

Micky never replied at first. He'd take the short black comb out of his back pocket and comb his hair; he'd do his nails on one hand with the nails of the other. He'd look grim and unsmiling just past Billy Thrower, as though whatever response he gave had implications. And then he'd answer.

"Naw," he'd say. "It's a bad night for it." As though he had special information that the place was going to blow up or be raided for back-room drug dealing.

Micky Olman was sweet to Rebecca and to no one else.

"He likes the fact your father's in jail," Billy Thrower said one night on the beach. "It turns him on."

"You like it too," Rebecca said. "You talk about it

164

all the time, like it's my major attraction for you."

"Well," he said, pulling her down, "there's other things I like about you too."

"Just don't mention my father again," she said, slipping from underneath him, getting up and walking through the low brush into the woods behind the beach. "I'm taking a walk," she said.

"A terrific idea and very timely."

"Alone," she said.

"I guessed it," Billy Thrower said. "Nervous girls drive me nuts," he said and buried his head in his arms, so he didn't see Micky Olman follow Rebecca into the woods. Rebecca was sitting on the ground, leaning against a tree, when Micky found her. She wasn't surprised to see him, as though they'd made arrangements, and she felt like other women she'd seen with the boys from New Canaan who knew what to do with their sex. She felt like a character in a movie.

Micky lay down beside her, took up a stick and talked to her, running the stick up and down her thighs.

"You like Billy?"

That was how the conversation started.

"Dunno," Rebecca said. "He's okay, I guess." Then she added, "Sort of," knowing that by dismissing Billy she was asking for trouble.

"What I mean is, do you have something between you?"

"Like what?"

"Like." He snapped her leg sharply with a stick.

"Like love," she added, provoking. "Or you mean like sex?"

Micky Olman was kissing her when Billy found them. Just sitting next to her beside the tree, kissing her.

"It was nothing," she said to Billy after he went for Micky's chin.

"Nothing," he said. "Ten or twelve a night? A regular girl wonder."

He was lying on his stomach. He had missed Micky when he lunged at him, and lay there on the ground, watching Micky clatter through the low brush back onto the beach.

He pulled Rebecca down next to him and kissed her hard. He flung his body on top of hers and rocked.

She didn't resist. She didn't enjoy this, but she didn't resist either, because she knew that this time she had pressed Billy Thrower too far and that a boy like him, without imagination or intelligence, could harm her.

Satisfied, he rolled over on his back and slept. When she finally woke him and dragged him back to the beach, everyone else had left and Billy's car was the only one in the parking lot.

"I have to go," she said. "I have to work tomorrow."

"You've got a late date on the next shift?"

She didn't realize he had drunk too much until he drove the car straight into the chain across the parking lot.

"Fuckers," he said.

"Didn't you see it?" she asked.

"Of course I saw it," he said. "But the damned thing stayed in my way." He leaned his head against the back seat and closed his eyes.

"You're bringing me bad luck," he said. "Lousy luck all the time."

She opened the car door. "I'll go," she said.

"Good idea."

"I'm sorry about the bad luck."

"Just leave me alone."

"I'll leave you alone."

"I think I'm a little too drunk to drive you home."

"Okay," she said.

"Good luck and all that," he said.

"You too."

When she looked at him from the street lights above Beach Drive, he was sleeping.

* * *

She walked home through the sleeping streets of Old Greenwich, past the house where she had grown up, dark over the Sound, but she felt it there as though it was a familiar presence which would take her in without question if she needed it, past the Barbers' house with the lights off, Johnny Barber off to college now, and by the rectory of Christ Church and the Ryans' house, the station wagon in the drive with a YALE sticker already—down Main Street, where in the distance above Aikens' Drugs she could see a light, which was either a street light or the light in her bedroom, where Sarah and Eric were waiting up for her.

18

Eric was cooking breakfast. Rebecca could hear the soft clatter of dishes in the kitchen, the purposeful smack of his tennis shoes against the linoleum. She could smell coffee burning and the sweet fragrance of cooked bread. It was early, just sunup, and the bedroom she shared with Sarah was bright with early autumn light and the rare quiet of morning before the work traffic began outside their window.

"Are you awake?" she asked Sarah. Sarah's eyes were closed, but she nodded, stretched above the sheets.

Rebecca threw off her covers, got up and sat on the side of the bed.

"What did you do yesterday?"

"Nothing," Sarah said. "Practiced. Took Liza to stay at Leuders' for the weekend."

"Did you see Daddy?" Rebecca sat cross-legged so her knees touched Sarah's. She had never noticed how black Sarah's eyes were in the light, how her skin was smooth as painted ocher.

"Yup," Sarah said. "I went with Eric."

"How was he?" Rebecca asked.

"Fine. As usual."

"Did he ask about me?"

Sarah closed her eyes again, rubbed them as if there was dust caught under the lid.

"Well?" Rebecca asked.

"Nope," Sarah said.

"Maybe he's given up on me."

"Maybe," Sarah said.

With Sarah's face quiet as it was just now, relaxed, not set for combat, she looked like Alicia Walker, just like her pictures when she was a child. Unexpectedly Rebecca reached over and touched her sister's cheek, as if to test the likeness.

"You look like Mother," she said.

"Do I?" Sarah asked.

"When you're quiet, you look exactly like her."

Sarah held her face just the way she had it, got up and looked in the mirror over her dresser.

"In the eyes, I guess," she said.

"It's more than that. It's the expression too. You have a hard expression when you're dancing."

Sarah collapsed back on the bed.

"You always liked Daddy best, didn't you?"

"Not best," Rebecca said. "I felt more like him. Related. I never felt that way with Mother."

"That's how I felt with Mother. Related," Sarah said and let her hand fall on top of her sister's hand as if by accident, and left it there.

There was an alteration in the spirit in the room, as

though an invisible composer had discovered by accident a new musical chord.

"I'm not going to see Billy Thrower again," Rebecca said. "Or any of the rest of the group from New Canaan."

"Did something happen?" Sarah asked.

"Not what you think," Rebecca said. She lay down beside her sister, propped her chin up. "I wanted it to, but it never did." Sometimes, lying on the beach next to Billy Thrower, she wanted to be over-whelmed, like the ocean overwhelms close to shore, knocked down by a huge wave, ground face down in the sand, fighting to keep her place as the water dragged her back with it.

"Almost," she said.

"You kissed lots of them?" Sarah asked.

"Only Billy Thrower and someone named Micky," she said and laughed. "Mother would have died if she'd seen Micky."

"What about Daddy?"

Rebecca didn't reply.

"You only kissed them?" Sarah asked.

"I said I didn't sleep with them," Rebecca said, "but of course I did more than kiss them."

Rebecca had been a cautious child when she was small, but once or twice she tested her changes. She remembered once lighting a match when she was four or five.

"Never," her mother had said, of course. "Never play with matches."

But she had found a pack of matches in her room,

left by her father, and decided to light just one and blow it out quickly. Which she did. But the pack of matches was full, and when she lit her one match with the pack open, the whole pack blazed instantly in her hands.

She burned a black hole in her rug where she had dropped the pack, beating out the fire with her sandals, and afterwards she moved her doll bed over the burned rug so no one would see it. She never told her mother, and when Alicia found the black hole, Rebecca said she didn't know how it got there. She did tell Eric once.

"Stupid," Eric said.

"I know," Rebecca said.

"Were you scared?"

"For a minute," she said, then added truthfully, "but it was fun too."

At first she had been frightened, in over her head with a small mistake, her heart beating too fast, but then she'd sat on her bed in her room with a strange thrill at the risk she'd taken. She felt that way now, lying on the bed with Sarah.

"Don't do it again," Eric had told her. "Or I'll tell."

"Eric told Daddy," Sarah was saying, "about the New Canaan group."

"He would."

"Eric thought you were trying to ruin yourself."

Rebecca shrugged. "Maybe so," she said. "What did Daddy say?"

"He said a funny thing." She sat up and crossed

171

her legs. "He said those boys were probably a lot like he used to be when he grew up in Brooklyn."

Rebecca rolled over on her back, folded her arms under her head for support.

"I never thought of that," she said. "You're sure he wasn't mad?" she asked.

"Not at all," Sarah said. "He seemed very matter-of-fact."

"Not silent like he gets when he's upset?"

"No," Sarah said. "How come? Do you want him to be upset with you?"

"Maybe so," Rebecca said. And she did. She wanted her father to know every detail of these last dreadful weeks, to see her with Billy Thrower for himself so there could be no mistake.

"I could have died," Rebecca said. "Not like Eric, either. I mean really died."

The night before walking through the streets of Old Greenwich away from the car blocked by the parking-lot chain where Billy Thrower lay drunk and asleep, Rebecca was conscious of danger, as though the familiar streets were unreliable at night. On Main Street she had begun to run. Later, trying to sleep but too wrought for sleeping, she knew that the dangers were not in the street of Old Greenwich but in herself. It was a mad game she had been playing with the boys from New Canaan. She didn't have their dark knowledge of a different world. She didn't know how to drink. She could have died on one of the back roads between New Canaan and Old Greenwich any night these last months with drunken Billy Thrower weaving those roads as though he were part of a balancing act.

Sarah put her head in Rebecca's lap.

"I used to think you were so good," Sarah said. "Sometimes I wanted something awful to happen to you."

Eric called them from the kitchen.

"Tell Eric I'm sleeping late," she said. "I don't have to work until noon." She crawled back in bed and lay down covering her eyes from the sun with her arm.

"I have to practice," Sarah said. "Are you going out tonight?"

"Nope."

"Are you mad about Yale?" Sarah asked.

"A little," Rebecca said. "You don't think you'll go to New York?"

"I'll finish high school here first," Sarah said. She leaned down and kissed Rebecca's forehead.

"Do you think this has been awful?"

"This year?" Rebecca laughed. "For hard-line addicts of tragedy like us, it's been a blast." She squeezed Sarah's hand.

* * *

In Rebecca's dream, her father was young and people said he looked exactly like her, remarked that they were like brother and sister. They smiled at her and her father when they rode by on their bikes, Edward first, pedaling without effort, his hair blown back, and Rebecca behind him, pedaling hard to keep up. There were cheers through the streets they were riding, as though it was a race, and as the dream progressed the distance between them grew wider until, hard as Rebecca pedaled, Edward Walker was only a dot in the distance and finally nothing at all. She rode on, following the place he had been, and the road narrowed and stopped at a chain similar to the one into which Billy Thrower had crashed the night before. When she got off her bike to look for him in the woods beyond the chain, like the woods beyond the beach where she had gone with Micky Olman, she discovered only Billy Thrower, face down, drunk and asleep.

"Have you seen my father?" she asked him.

"Leave me alone."

"Leave me alone," she yelled and recognized the sound of her own voice.

"Gladly," Eric said. "It'll be a real pleasure." He was sitting beside her on the bed. "If you'll stop screaming."

She sat up in bed.

"I was screaming?" she asked.

"I don't usually shake you awake in the morning, I should point out," he said.

"I was having a dream."

Eric got up, looked out on Main Street at Mrs. Leuders with her marketing.

"I hope it's not the beginning of a new tradition," he said.

"It was about Daddy." She shook her head to get

174

rid of the memory of dreaming. "What was I screaming? Can you remember?"

"Yeah," Eric said, picking up the clothes she had
thrown down the night before. "You were screaming
for Dad."

19

Alicia Walker was coming home.

"She's well," Sarah said, doing a cartwheel through the center of the room. "Well, well, well."

"Better," Rebecca said carefully.

"Will she look the same?" Eliza asked.

"She looked beautiful when I saw her," Sarah said.

"Is her hair long?" Eliza asked. "Does she still wear that bathrobe all the time?"

"Her hair is long, long, long." Sarah went across the room on her toes. "And she was wearing a dress and stockings, like a regular woman, like an ordinary mother, only much more beautiful."

"Can you talk to her?" Rebecca asked. "Really talk with her?"

"You can," Sarah said. "I did. She was nearly the same as she was before Daddy, only a little as though she had fallen and had the breath knocked out."

"I found a house," Eric said, walking in the apartment in a blue suit and striped tie, looking better than he had in months, as though he would outlast his middle age. "It's a working-class bungalow on Lincoln, but it's a house with a yard and windows, bathrooms, doors, recognizable by anyone as a house where ordinary respectable people might live."

"Respectable people like us." Eliza jumped up and hugged her brother.

"Like us, for example," Eric said and swung his youngest sister around.

"Did you buy it?" Sarah asked.

"I stole it, darling," Eric said. "It was quite simple. No one was looking."

* * *

Actually Patty Miller found the house on Lincoln Avenue first, because it belonged to a friend of hers who had bought it as an investment. As a favor the friend agreed to rent the house cheaply to the Walkers as long as they would fix it up.

"I have found just the place," Patty told Eric when she called. "But you won't like the color. It's barn red."

"I don't care," Eric said, "as long as it's a house."

"It's a house, but the neighborhood's transient," Patty went on. "The people next door are from Ohio."

"I'm a tolerant man, Patty. I think I can live next door to people from Ohio," Eric said. "Is it cheap?"

"Very," Patty said. "That's the good thing. It's inexpensive, but the kitchen's too small."

"We'll take it in spite of the people from Ohio and the kitchen," Eric said. "We've given up eating, anyway, since Gayatri left."

* * *

177

Alicia Walker was coming home to a house, a shingle bungalow with shutters and a tiny yard, but a yard at least and a room to herself, two blocks north of the house where she grew up. With the windows open you could hear the Sound on a quiet day.

The Walker children spent all day Saturday and Sunday scrubbing and painting the bungalow in white and sunny yellow, the colors of spring. They borrowed the truck from Aikens' Drugs to move the furniture themselves, and bought flowers for all the rooms from Mrs. Johnson.

"We're moving to a new house," Eliza told Mrs. Johnson, "and my mother is well, and by October my father can be on parole."

"Is that true?" Rebecca asked Eric.

"About Daddy?"

"I thought he'd be in prison eighteen months before parole."

"You hoped," Eric said, carrying down lamps and boxes from the apartment to the truck.

"I can't live in a house with him," Rebecca said.

"By spring you can go to Yale."

"It's not soon enough," she said, helping him with the mattress.

* * *

When they were settled in the new house with all the furniture and lamps in place, when the beds were made and the refrigerator full and the cabinets stacked with dishes, when the sun had gone down on the last day before Alicia Walker's return, the Walker children sat down for a supper celebration.

"Just the four of us," Eric said. He lifted his wine glass solemnly. "To the Walker children," he said.

"Will it be the same as it used to be when we lived on the Sound?" Eliza asked.

"It'll never be the same again, because we're different," Rebecca said.

"And it'll be dull because I'm going back to Cambridge on Tuesday."

"You can't stand to be healthy any longer," Rebecca said, "so you're going back to Gayatri."

"Listen, Rebecca," Eric said, rolling up his sleeves and pointing to a fat mosquito bite. "Fifteen percent of the mosquitoes in the northeastern United States carry encephalitis."

"Brain damage," Rebecca said. "You'd better go back to Cambridge."

* * *

Rebecca couldn't sleep in the new house. She got out of bed and went into the living room, where Eric was reading.

"It's after twelve," he said.

"I can't sleep."

"Excited?"

"I guess," she said. She sat down on the couch across from him. "Are Sarah and Liza asleep?"

"I presume," he said. "I can't sleep, either."

"So you decided to read up on diseases."

She closed her eyes. In the light with Eric there, she felt sleepy.

"I wonder," she said, "what Daddy thinks of me now?"

179

"Ask him."

"He knows about this summer, doesn't he?" she asked.

"Your low-life companions."

She nodded.

"Sure, he knows."

"Did he say anything?"

"Go see him, Rebecca," Eric said. "Give him a chance to say something."

"I wonder," she said, lying down on the couch, closing her eyes, "what he can say."

"The question is whether you'll forgive him," Eric said.

That was the question which had kept Rebecca from sleeping, not just this night but other nights. She tossed between the sheets and listened to the gentle breathing of her sisters—wide-awake in the darkness, thinking of Billy Thrower and her life this summer, of the risks she had taken.

She remembered the first time she had returned home after a long trip and the house on the Sound seemed smaller than her memory of it or else she had grown in the weeks of separation. She wanted to recapture the old dimensions, but they were lost to her, as though they had only been imagined.

"I will never feel the same way about him as I did when I believed he was innocent," Rebecca said.

"Of course not," Eric said.

"Or when I was young."

"You shouldn't feel like you used to feel about him, because it wasn't true," Eric said. "He's an ordinary man who made a large mistake, but he's not a bad man."

"I suppose," Rebecca said.

"I think you can forgive at least in a small way an ordinary man who is your father."

"I don't know," she said. "Stupidly, I had thought that if we got through this, our lives could be the same again."

"Never," he said. "Something is lost in growing up for everyone."

She wanted to ask her brother if he understood why she had been courting disaster this summer, but they were both too raw-nerved for personal talk especially in a family that had learned to carefully protect their sensibilities with sharp conversation.

Eric put his textbook under the light.

"It says here the symptoms of encephalitis appear shortly after you've been bitten and start with a headache, which I have."

Rebecca put her hands over her ears.

* * *

Alicia Walker was coming home on Monday afternoon, and Rebecca took the day off.

Sarah and Eliza sat on the bed and watched Rebecca dress in a blue denim skirt and rose shirt and then a white skirt and the rose shirt and then a blue silk shirt with an open collar and then a flowered dress, settling finally on the dress.

"Don't you think it looks best?" she asked, looking at herself in the mirror.

"For Mother coming home?" Sarah asked. "Let's look regular. I'm wearing shorts."

"Me too," said Eliza.

"I'm not getting dressed up for Mother. I'll change to shorts when she gets here," Rebecca said. "I'm going to the prison."

* * *

"Did you know?" Sarah asked Eric.

"Yeah," Eric said. "But don't make a big deal."

Eric had known last night, talking with Rebecca in the living room after the others were asleep. He'd looked up at her once when she didn't notice him looking, when her face was at ease, and there lingered in it, in her eyes especially, an expression which he remembered as the young child Rebecca Walker before these last months. She had been, he thought to himself, too good a girl.

* * *

Rebecca drove to Bridgeport in Patty Miller's car so she could be back in time to meet Alicia.

"Take it," Patty had said intensely. "All day if you need it. Tomorrow," she said. "All week." And Rebecca left quickly before Patty wept.

"Poor Patty," Rebecca said to Eric. "Our family's problems are too much for her."

"Perhaps we should keep the car permanently if it would make her feel better," Eric said. "I could take it to Cambridge."

Rebecca left at nine. She took the Post Road, the slow way, past the Main Street shops, just opening

Monday morning, the school children crossing with patrols, the packing and supply trucks blocking the right lane, the last of the commuter traffic to New York, on bicycles, in cars, ill-tempered at stoplights. She took the slow way to prepare to see her father, to imagine conversations they would have, to rehearse her lines. But she had decided before she even left Old Greenwich that if she thought on the way to New Canaan, she would turn around with Patty Miller's car, park it in front of the gray shingle house on the Sound and go home. Instead she looked in shop windows and at children going to school, choosing one to watch in a red plaid skirt, an old-fashioned child with braids and a book bag already full of books in September. She watched the red-haired woman at a stoplight light the wrong end of her cigarette and swear. She watched a young and handsome man stretch across a baby in a car seat to kiss his wife goodbye. By the time she had pulled into the parking lot in Bridgeport, she hadn't allowed herself a chance to think at all. She got out of the car, ran her hand through her hair, rubbed her cheeks for color and went straight to the visiting room without stopping to reconsider.

Edward Walker was standing in the visiting room of the prison when Rebecca arrived. He was looking out the window at the parking lot full of police cars or at the trees beyond, which circled a park where children played with their mothers, perhaps hearing stories from them of the prisoners, with warnings of the dark future for children who misbehaved.

"Hello," Rebecca said quickly before he had a chance to know that she was there, to turn around and catch her open and unguarded face.

"I'm finally here."

SUSAN SHREVE has quickly established herself as an unusually gifted writer for young people and adults. Her books for young people are *The Nightmares of Geranium Street, Loveletters* and *Family Secrets* (all Knopf); her most recent adult novel is *Children of Power*. A graduate of the University of Pennsylvania, she is an associate professor of English at George Mason University. Susan Shreve lives with her husband and their four children in Washington, D.C.